Taking Out

Chapter 1.

Her thin, arthritic fingers struggled to tie the wispy string around the top of the black, plastic sack. She only had to get it to the bin outside the back door, Harry would take it from there. Harry was a good man, he understood her frailties, considerate, cheerful an ever-helpful soul.

"Tibby! You'll be the death of me!" She gently shooed the handsome tabby from under her feet, as she pulled the weighted bag towards the door. Tutting to herself, she realised she'd forgotten to remind Harry to pop a bulb in the outside light.

Her eyesight wasn't what it was, she carefully lowered herself and the heavy bag down the three steps. One hand tightly on the rail, wasn't quite enough, as the weight of the bag swung forward, pulling her off balance, heart pounding she managed to stop herself from falling.

She'd shrunk so much with age everyday tasks had become such a struggle. Her tiny frame pained from such, that in her youth, would have taken her seconds to do. Back inside, she held the sink side to catch her breath. Still aching she turned slowly back to the door. Lock, bolt, top, middle, bottom, mortice lock and finally the chain, she never forgot.

Arthur and she used to joke about their failings. What one couldn't manage, the other could. He would thread her needles, as her eyesight failed and she would listen out for 'Gardeners Question Time', then turn the radio up, pretending she'd just realised the time, knowing he wouldn't hear at normal   volume.

Till death us do part and it had, cruelly and painfully for both.

She thought her heart would break as she watched him take his last breath. She had tried to stay strong, telling him over and over how much she loved him, he'd then squeezed her hand one last time. His pain was gone, but hers had only just begun. Her love, her husband, her best friend, the emptiness consumed her at times, two years on and she still missed him, with all her heart.

"Come on girl, where's your fighting spirit." She said out loud, remembering his words of encouragement. "We got through the blitz, we can manage a bit of cleaning and a couple of hanging baskets, eh love?" She smiled and stood as straight as her painful back would allow.

"Right Tibby, where's your partner in crime? Monty! Supper time! Minced cod and shrimp. You two are eating better than me these days."

A large, portly black and white cat, with markings that gave him the look of wearing a waistcoat and a rather off-centre moustache, sauntered through to the kitchen. Both cats, curling themselves gently around Doris's knees, purring loudly as she put a large spoonful of cat food in their respective bowls.

As they tucked into supper, Doris turned off the little heater by her chair in the front room, tucking her knitting back inside the cloth bag, she turned off the lights. With Arthur gone it was even more important to save the pennies.

The silence was broken by the phone ringing. Smiling, she picked up the receiver. "Gran! It's Jamie. Thank you so much! A car for our twenty-first! Mum and dad said you put in some money for it, you shouldn't have, but thanks ever so much. We'll be able to drive to Uni, no more trains and coaches!"

"You lucky boys, which half is yours then?" She asks with a laugh. The phone then crackles.

"Gran! It's me....Dan. I've told Jamie he can drive, I'll just lounge on the backseat, with a few beautiful hitchhikers!"

For a moment Doris was whisked back 62 years when she met Arthur. She was twenty, he was twenty-two. He'd learnt to drive in the army and was home on leave, driving his father's Austin. He'd seen her struggling with her suitcase out of Middlesbrough station, on her way to Auntie Flo's for Easter. He'd pulled up and offered her a lift, her heart had fluttered, as his eyes caught hers. It was all so innocent then. Kids nowadays disappear, hitch lifts, get taken away by awful people with so much evil on their minds.

"Gran...you okay?" Dan sounded concerned at her silence. "Of course lovey" he heard her chuckle.

"I'd better go Gran, mum wants a word, she's hovering, doing her usual manic semaphore! Love you Gran, see you in the hols." This is echoed by Jamie.

"Love to you too boys. Are you there Hetty love?"

"Mum...How's your back? Sorry about the boys ringing so late, they're just so excited about the car. Just seemed a waste to keep them from using it till June. They're doing so well at Uni, thought it would keep them motivated. Not that we'd have managed without your contribution mum, Russell and I are so grateful, we will pay you back."

"Hetty, you and Russell and the twins are my world. Your dad felt the same.

The boys are good lads, they push themselves, not like some of the terrible looking things I pass when I go to the Post Office...." She stopped herself knowing this would give Hetty something else to worry and feel guilty about.

"Oh mum! I wish you'd come and live with us, if we could move up there, we would, but Russell can't afford to lose this job, or his pension. We could pop up on Saturday, Russ can put up that extra shelf in the pantry and I could get you a bit of shopping, save you going over the precinct. You don't speak to those people, do you? You've locked up properly haven't you mum? I do worry...."

"Hetty love, I wish you wouldn't worry, I'm fine, I locked up after I put the rubbish out. Harry will take the bin from the back door...."

Hetty interrupts. "Which is Harry again mum? Is he the dustbin man, who's mum died same time as dad, he seems kind, is that him?"

"Yes love, nursed his old mum, like I did your father, right to the end. He's a good man with a kind heart. He's going to pop me a new bulb in the outside......"

She realised she'd done it again. "Oh mum! You mean there's no light down the path to the back door?"

"Hetty! Stop worrying, it's like Fort Knox here. I don't want to move, this is me and your dad's home, always will be. Anyway, Tibby and Monty keep me company and I talk to your dad all the time. If I'm losing me marbles, I'd rather it was only the cats to witness it!"

She began quickly thinking of more reassurance for her daughter.

"There's Mrs Elliott up the road and Maude's always popping in, I'm fine here. I'm off to bed now love, Tibby and Monty are off upstairs, they'll take over the bed if I'm not up there sharpish. Give my love to Russ and the boys...night Hetty love."

"Okay, take care. I'll give you a ring tomorrow, love you mum."

Doris, smiling tiredly, climbed the stairs. Old age was such a terrible, unforgiving time of life. Physically everything was getting slower, weaker and wrinklier.

When had her skin turned to tissue paper? Blotchy, crepey, hunched and frail, that's all people saw her as. But inside she felt no different to that young woman who had fallen in love, that danced the nights away, worked hard for years, gave birth to two stillborn babies, then finally to their beautiful daughter, Henrietta, while the war raged on and she waited for Arthur's safe return. The joyful memories of walking with Arthur and Hetty, making sandcastles, riding ponies, cycling in the hills......now she could barely get up her own stairs to her bed.

Doris took a clean nightie and towel from the warm airing cupboard, as she crossed the landing. The cats had beaten her to the bed, she squeezed in gently without disturbing them. The water bottle she'd popped in earlier

9

was still warm as she slid her cold, aching feet under the covers.

It was ten to eleven, she wound the clock slowly while gazing at her two favourite photographs. Arthur, looking handsome in his army uniform and Doris in a dress her mum had made, out of Aunt Winnie's lobby curtains, 'make do and mend' it was then. Get it on HP or steal it, that seems to be how it is nowadays.

The other photo was Arthur, looking chipper on his 80th birthday, before ill-health struck. Still had those twinkling eyes, handsome as ever, sitting proudly with his doting family around him.

Doris let tiredness take over, she leant back on the pillows, carefully tipped two white pills into her mouth, sipped some water and hoped for a pain free night.

"Goodnight Arthur love. Expect you know about the boy's car, a mini. That'll be another thing for Hetty to worry about!"

She chuckled to herself. Poor Russell, he does his best to keep her mind off things. They could pop over Saturday, stop Hetty fretting.

"Right love, time Dotty got some beauty sleep." She smiled as her eyes closed, tiredness overwhelming her.

"Don't forget Arthur, when it's time for you to come for me...while asleep and wearing a clean nightie......that's me, not you, silly old fool. Love you Arthur

Linton.... dearest Arthur"....

Chapter 2

"Where yer off to, yer little tosser?" The thin, agitated male, heading from the stairs and out the front door, turned and glared towards the front room, as he passed the angry vision. "Mind yer own, yer fat git!"

The large male wearing a grubby vest, baggy sweatpants, was trying his best to get up from his chair, puffy and spluttering. "Why don't you push-off back to where you came from, and I want me money back before you disappear you thieving shit!"

Within minutes, Liam was rushing down the stairs.

"Dad! Will yer just leave it! Dabber will 'av yer money, soon as. Just give him a chance to find a bit of work for Christ's sake."

His father was still struggling, like a netted whale. "Him! Fuckin' work! Yer 'avin a laugh aren't yer,

13

scrounging waster!" Liam pushes Dabber out the door to stop him making a lunge towards the front room.

"We're off down the town, tell mam not to wait up, right." The heavy bulk had just managed to get out of the chair as the door shut. He continued to shout at the closed door. "Where the fuck you off to at this pissing time 'o night anyway, it's after eleven? If that tosser gets you into any trouble, I'll lynch the bastard....I will! Druggie piece of shite.......

He's probably hiding up here anyway...he'll owe money down there I bet!......Bloody little......!"

The kitchen door suddenly flies open, the smell of cigarette smoke and old chip fat fills the room. "For Christs sake man, will yer shut yer yap, get this down yer neck yer whinging git."

A raddled, female appears, in tight, grubby pink velour trousers, a sweat stained vest. Hair scraped back, her skin lined and dry, a dark shade of Hazelnut fake tan. She proffers a large plate, piled high with sausage and chips.

"Our Liam told me earlier he was going down Boro, t'meet some mates and Stacey."

Earl slams the arm of the chair. "Silly sod's not still with that slapper is he? She's bleeding him dry, there's no way that kid is his! The lying tramp! Three bloody kids, t'other fathers aren't paying out. Just cos our Liam's a decent lad wi' a bit a work coming his way. Kyle's not his, look at the bairn's hair! Black and curly, our Liam's is straight as…..."

She leans forward. "Well, just shows how little you were around when our Liam was a bairn then dunnit. Look!" She thrusts a nicotine, stained photo, in an elaborate frame, into his face.

"He wa' 3-year-old there! Thick, black, curly hair! Where were you?! Fucking Durham Prison, that's where!

15

What the fuck would you know about the bairns! You weren't here half the time and when yer were, yer wa' either drunk out yer skull, or giving me another little arse t'wipe."

"Ah! Yer love me though, don't yer doll? Fancy coming over 'ere and sharing me sausage, eh?" Mim snorted loudly, lighting up another cigarette.

"O 'ay, hang on pet, you eat yer chips, I'll just finish me fag, then yer can 'av me on the hearth rug if you can get yer lardy arse out that chair."

He begins to cram his slavering mouth with chips as he leers at her. "Give us ten minutes doll, I'll be in there, don't you worry."

She wasn't worried. Twenty minutes later Mim stubs out another cigarette, closes her magazine and walks in from the kitchen, Earl is prostrate in the chair, full of sausage, chips, four cans of lager and snoring loudly.

Dabber still angry from Earl's tirade, kicks a fence in passing.

"Christ, Liam man, how do you put up wi' Earl, I fuckin' hate the bastard!"

Liam smiles, shaking his head. "He's just an old lardy arse, his barks worse than his bite. He was a bloody hard man in his day mate. He's all talk now."

Liam knew his dad was ill, past his best, couldn't do much of anything now.

He'd heard mam telling Noreen, he couldn't get it up anymore, nothing for six years.

Six bloody years! Poor sod. He'd feel frustrated if it were six days! Mind you the thought of Stacey getting pregnant again had put him right off. She'd sworn the last time that she was on the pill. Probably mistook the contraceptive pill for ecstasy, or whatever else she pops when she's out with the lasses. She was beginning to get him down. He kept bailing her out for Kyle's sake, but she just kept spending.

Suddenly Dabber bounced in front of Liam, as they walked towards the corner to flag down a taxi. "Right mate, what's happening tonight, is your Stacey bringing that Dominique bird with'er? She'ad a pair on 'er, I could do with some er that like." Dabber rearranged his crotch area. "That tight little cow wouldn't give it the other night, I spent a bloody fortune in that club. She wouldn't come outside, so I tried to get er in the corner for a bit of a, Dabber dabble, she was 'avin none of it, frigid cow! Who wouldn't want a bit of the 'Mighty Dabber' eh mate?" His bouncing turned to a smug, swaggering gait.

As their taxi pulled up near the town hall, Liam caught sight of Stacey. The huge gold hooped earrings, she'd insisted he buy her, glinting in the streetlight. She was wearing one of those tiny skirts, it barely covered the

18

inadequate piece of material she called pants, her arse cheeks on display every time she lunged forward to screech with laughter. Her top barely covered her tits and that horrible fake tan stuff all over. He looked at her clanking towards him and wished Kyle had been born to anyone else but her, poor little sod, he had no chance.

"Liam! Where the fuck 'av yer bin? We've bin' waiting bloody ages! I've got to get back fer twelve like." Liam muttered under his breath something about it being too late she'd already turned into a pumpkin. "Our Julie sez she's not staying any later, cos she's already 'ad the bairns three times this week, stingy cow."

Liam stopped in his tracks. "You were supposed to be saving money! I thought you said only Thursday with me and Saturday with the lasses, till you'd paid off Brickhead?"

Stacey's face came out at him like a gurning tortoise. "Yeh! Well, you'd like me to stay in wouldn't yer. Wasting me fuckin' life away, in some poxy flat with a load of kids. I can't help it if I want some fun. Brickhead will just 'av t'wait for his money, won't he!"

He stared at her. "You had a choice to have kids, you silly bitch, thick or what!

I paid Brickhead off last time Stacey, I am not doing it again! I'm going away on a job. Then you'll be out every night! Then they'll send the bloody bailiffs in! Just cut down for a couple of months, Stacey, it'll be nowt compared to the life you'll have in debt, with Brickhead on yer case." Liam knew he was wasting his breath.

Dabber was becoming agitated again, hopping from one foot to the other.

"For fucks sake will yer stop arguing......the pair of yers!" Dabber had quickly moved his eyes from them to the chest area of the young girl next to Stacey.

"Who's this then Stace?" He leaned towards her slightly, sniffing her like an animal on heat.

"You a'right gorgeous!" He carried on leering at the young girl. Liam looked at him with disdain.

"This is our Kendra and yer can keep yer mucky thoughts to yer'sel. She's me Aunt Gwen's oldest. Our Gwen's just 'ad another bairn to some pervy shit that was trying to get into our Kendra's knickers while Gwen were up the duff like. So, our mam said she could stay with us."

"You'll want a good night out then.........Kendra love, eh?" Dabber moves closer to the girl sliding his arm around her skinny frame.

"She's fourteen, yer fuckin pervert, she's 'ad enough of dirty gits like you." Dabber winks at the girl, who is sadly, looking slightly impressed by Dabber's lecherous efforts. "Well, she's got to learn sometime, why not let Dabber show you some moves." Liam glares at him.

Liam then makes a grab for Stacey's hand. "Let's just go for a drink and a bit of food eh?" Dabber then squeezes Kendra, deftly moving his hand up under her jacket to cop a feel. "I know what I'd like to be eating later, eh Kendra?" Kendra giggles.

Liam points a finger at Dabber in threat. "Only jokin' mate, can't 'elp if the lasses fancy me like.......l am the Mighty Dabber!"

Albert Road is heaving with revellers, the music is pulsing, the pubs are crammed.

Liam pushes his way to the bar. "Get me a Slammer babe, get me in the mood eh?" Stacey then bites his neck and squeezes his buttock. Liam winces.

"Thought your Julie wanted you back for twelve."

Stacey slides her leg between his. "Well, she's gonna' av t'wait." He feels her hand slide to the front of his trousers. "Your Stace is   feeling a bit horny babe."

Liam pulls away quickly. He whispers loudly. "Do you have to be so full-on. I just want a quiet drink. I'm going up Newcastle tomorrow, early doors, Benny's got some work for me, I need to make some cash." Liam catches her look, as he pays the barman.

Stacey glaring at him, picks up her drink. He knows it won't be coming his way, she wouldn't waste good alcohol. "Right well, you fuckin' av yer early night, yer boring bastard! Your loss! Me and our Kendra are off wi' lasses to 'av some fun...yer remember that do yer....fun?" She grabs Kendra's arm, pulling away her from Dabber's grasp.

Dabber obviously now frustrated and angry. "What the fuck did yer do that for?

I was in there, man. I could av 'ad her, could hav 'ad her man!"

"Will yer shut-up Dabber! Go and have a wank man, yer doing me head in, yer bloody obsessed!" He just needed to get out of here, fast. Not just the pub, his home, his relationship, this area, his situation, his life, the whole bloody lot, he just wanted out.

"Look...I'm off...I'm off out of here mate, I'm going home to pack some stuff. I'm going for that job tonight. I need to sort me head out, right?"

Dabber wasn't listening, frustration and the sweats were taking over. "Yeh...Right mate...yer off...yeah, yer couldn't just lend us some dosh mate...for a fix mate...... twenty 'ull do like...yeh?"

Liam takes out a twenty. "Couldn't make it forty...yer know...just till I get me giro, yeh?" Liam pulls back, shoving the twenty in Dabber's hand.

"No way! I need the rest. Say nout t' Stacey right. I'll send something for Kyle to me mam when I get sorted, okay?"

"Are you sure that fucking kids yours mate?" Liam turned to walk away.

"Don't you fuckin' start! I've 'ad it with all this, I'm off!... See yer around."

Dabber began squeezing his way through the scantily clad girls chatting around the bar, his hands sliding round their tight backsides, he couldn't resist thrusting forward slightly as he got caught behind a big-breasted blonde, just his type, but she turned on him.

"Bloody hell! You filthy perv! He's only got a fuckin' hard-on, yer dirty bastard! Can you believe it!" The girl swung round, trying to whack him with her bag, but he managed to duck.

He didn't manage to escape the bouncers though, who heard the commotion and man-handled him swiftly out the door. He saw a huge, black doorman, standing over him, looking at him with disgust. "Have some respect man. I know some of them dress a bit fresh, but they're still ladies, till proven otherwise. Get yourself down Snowden Road, or Union Street man, get yersel' sorted. We're a decent club here, look at the state of you man!"

Dabber scuttled off up Albert Road, then rolled instinctively back into an office doorway, as a blue light and sirens turns towards him from Borough Road, he muttered to himself. "Fuckin' cop-shop round the corner, won't be going that way." As he picks up pace across the well-lit town centre, the smell of takeaway food flares his nostrils with hunger. Which did he want more...food, fix, or a good fuck...difficult choice, if he played his cards right, maybe he could get all three.

He squinted as he stepped into the bright lights of The Kebab Kitchen.

"Large Donor, everything on it, right, plenty of them green and red things, yeh." The ever-patient staff check politely, pointing at the tubs. "You mean the chillies sir...?"

"What the fucks wrong wi'yer! If yer can't understand the lingo, fuck off back to where yer came from, I said, them things there, yeh!"

"I was born in Stockton-on-Tees and lived in Middlesbrough since the age of three and you sir?" Dabber was getting annoyed now. "I don't want yer fuckin' life story Abdul, just a fucking kebab! Nottingham! I come from Nottingham! Better than this poxy dump any day."

Maybe *you* would prefer to go back to where *you* came from then...sir?" Dabber could see his slight smile. "You wanna fuckin' make somethin' of it, like?"

"Good evening, Mr Haslam, is this gentleman giving you any problems?" Dabber turned to see the yellow fluorescent covered, body armour of a Police officer, towering above him.

"No, officer, I think the 'gentleman' was just leaving."

The Police officer, obviously looking into a familiar face, smiled wryly. "What brings you to the delights of Borough Road, Mr Dalby? You're usually doing a bit of pub hopping South Bank way?" Dabber had grabbed his kebab, picking at the contents, as he slid towards the door past the two officers, the last thing he needed was this lot to spoil his plans.

He picked up his change. "Just on me way, with me mates like, no bother officer, right." He couldn't resist making several snorting, pig noises as he left, walking quickly, just in case.

"Just because we wear helmets Dalby, doesn't make us deaf, same as you wearing that tracksuit doesn't make you an Olympic gold medallist, so if I were you, I'd get a head start." The other officer muffled his laughter, watching Dabber's pace quicken, as he continued to stuff the food hungrily into his mouth.

The Officers shaking their heads as the watch him scuttle away. "What does he think he looks like? Socks up over his trackies, that bloody cap, if he were on the 16th hole and that was in tartan, he'd still look a right clip!"

As he got onto Union Street, Dabber caught sight of one of Milo's boys, just coming out of Warren Street. He threw the rest of his kebab onto the pavement and rushed over.

"Yo! Red! It's Dabber mate, yer couldn't bung me a couple of tabs, or a bag for a tenner mate, yeh?" Red, so named possibly for the shock of red hair, not that anyone ever dared call him, 'ginger' and lived to brag about it, or it was rumoured, named 'Red' for the blood he'd spilt, as one of Milo's henchman. Looking at the huge frame, it wasn't something Dabber was going to question.

Red turned, walking towards a large dark blue BMW with blacked out windows, he taps the front passenger side, the electric window slides down.

"Fuck off Dabber, you still owe Milo."

Dabber leans forward to find himself looking into, the glinting Raybans of Lee Bailey, sitting in the passenger seat, adjusting her clothing, her eyes glazed, a young girl, he steps back hastily thrusting a note at Red.

"I've got a tenner, here now, look." He flaps the note at Red. "I'll sell for yer as pay back. Come down t'Langy reck tomorrow night, loads o' kids there. They're already thievin' at least they can 'ave a bit o' fun for the money."

He turns back to Red in desperation, as Lee shakes his head slowly with a look of disgust, he hears a sucking of teeth from the car, as the window whirs shut.

"You better give a return on this man, or yer a dead fucker, right?" Red passes him a small bag and snatches the tenner before Dabber runs.

"I owe yer man, right." Dabber rushes off, dipping into the shadows two streets up, his thin, shaking fingers barely able to open the bag, a dirty nailed digit delves into the white powder and he rubs it frantically onto his gums.

"Fucking 'ell...that's the dog's bollocks, man." He leans back on the wall letting it take over. "Now for a fuckin' good shag." He strides towards the business units, off Derwent Street. He squints into the dark doorways. He can see one of the prossies. Some of the young'uns will go all the way for a fiver. If it's an old bird, they'll just bring him off, if he's lucky.

"Jade, eh, is that you?" He asks, peering into the dark recess of a garage doorway. A small, thin woman steps out into the light, in a long, pale blue, padded anorak, arms folded tightly over her body against the cold night air.

"You lookin' for business luv?" He stares at the thin, bare legs, her worn down heels, the dark bags under her eyes, the inch of dark greasy hair disappearing into a straggly mess of straw yellow. Then catches sight of the low-slung tits, as she opens her coat for a couple of seconds, hoping that may make a difference to the transaction. He sighs ...needs must. "What can I get for a fiver."

She steps forward and almost spits at him. "A fucking taxi home mate, now piss off, or I'll shout me bloke over, yer tight shit!" Dabber almost trips back over the pavements edge, steadying himself and rearranging his crotch area, which is now feeling slightly less twitchy.

He strides off muttering to himself, but keeping an eye on the large pimp, who appears from behind the building, walking slowly towards him.

'Fuckin' ugly old cow, her loss, no dibble from the Dabber for 'er. Shit, now what. Maybe if I go round Kieron's, he'll let me doss down at his, caj a few quid. Maybe even 'ave his missus, she's always up for it and he's always pissed.'

Dabber smiles to himself, sets off at a good pace in the general direction of Kieron's, but all the streets look the same. He's usually with Liam, or others, when they go round for a smoke. He jumps the barriers near the school, it's over here somewhere. The road isn't familiar. He walks some way up, then trying to get his head together, sits down on a low, stone wall.

Must be late now, he turns to look at the house in darkness behind him, but the curtains are open. Maybe there's a clock he can see.

He sidles through the open gate and peers through the window, no clock, maybe round the back. He creeps, unseen in the darkness down the side path. He curses the net curtains in the kitchen window. "Bloody useless things, can't see nowt through 'em."

The backroom window has curtains closed part way, covering from the inside the small, top window which has been left open. He's thinking about it, staring at the window. This was easy for a skinny git like him. Would it be worth the effort though?

He wanted money, stuff to flog, maybe…you never know, even something worth shagging? He could feel the adrenaline, mixed with everything else, coursing through his body. He pulled from his pocket, his gloves. Why else was he known as,

'No Dabs Dabber'. Carefully, he balanced himself on the outside windowsill, then deftly up and through the small transom window. Going headfirst, he slithered, like a snake, dangling halfway, then down onto the inside sill, carefully moving an ornament, eyes quickly getting used to the darkness within. He had done this so many times now, it was second nature. He preferred them empty, last thing he needed was dogs, or pain in the arse have-a-go owners, trying to protect themselves and lunging at him with cricket bats, or frying pans.

His eyes focused as he picked up a magazine, on a nearby table, 'Peoples Friend'. His eyes darting around wildly he saw a large bag of knitting by a chair, covered in embroidered cats. "It's a fucking oldie again, just my bloody luck."

Chapter 3

Doris, half asleep, thought she heard a noise. She looked at the cats, they were still asleep. If they hadn't moved it was just her and her silly imagination. There hadn't been a burglary in this road for years. Mr Tomlin at number four had got his bicycle stolen, but that was from outside the post office.

But Monty then woke, his ears turned towards the door. Then Tibby sat up and stared in the same direction. Doris carefully reached for the bedside light, clicking it on. She then looked at her photos, then to the phone.

"What should I do Arthur. I'm being silly aren't I, not right to waste the poor Policemen's time if it's nothing." She whispered to herself, but then she heard a creak on the stairs. How many times had Arthur brought her up a cup of tea, or cocoa at bed-time, sixth and ninth stair up always creaked. Her heart began to pound her mouth went dry. She knew

Arthur had kept his old cricket bat under the bed, maybe...she could....maybe...if they knew someone was here, they would turn and go. Maybe if she just gave them some money they would go. Maybe........it was Arthur, his ghost.......any ghost.... would be better than....... Straining to hear.......she swallowed hard.

"Hello...is....is someone there?" Doris hoped, with all her heart that it was not the bad thing at the back of her mind that would happen next. She was trying so hard to control her fear. Monty's fur rose, he then jumped from the bed and ran out onto the landing. Doris cried out.

"Monty......Monty!" She clung to the bedclothes, now squashing herself back into the pillows, as she heard a sickening cry, then a thud.

"Fucking moggies, I hate 'em! Your fuckin' cat scratched me, well not anymore, the little fucker." Doris froze as the awfulness of what was in her home, had now stepped into her bedroom.

In the lamplight, the peak of his cap pulled well down was shadowing his face. He was small, rat-like. What her Arthur would call, 'the runt of the litter'.

He was thin, in one of those shapeless, tracksuit things. She tried to focus on his face. His mouth was moving, shouting, in a loud whisper, torrents of foul language. She had only ever heard Arthur swear twice. Both when he was in severe pain and neither word had been anything as abhorrent as what she was hearing now. She couldn't understand what she'd done to warrant this vile, verbal attack.

"What....what, do you want? I don't have anything of value."

Doris tried to stay calm, though her heart was pounding so hard she could hardly hear herself speaking, she felt weak with fear, she could feel herself shaking, from inside out.

"I know you oldies.........you 'ave fucking money stuffed away all oer'! Money! That's what I want first...then...well, we'll see what else takes me fancy eh? Know what I mean eh?" He leaned in towards her, leering. Doris felt physically sick. Surely, he couldn't mean...not that. She was 82 years old.

He walked into the room and started pulling drawers open, throwing the contents onto the floor, with total disregard. "Please stop, I might some money. But it's all I've got, it's in there." She carefully got up, her limbs shaking, she grabbed the arm of the chair and got herself to the wardrobe. Carefully turning the lock, she suddenly felt a searing pain across her forearm, as his fist came down in anger.

"See, l knew you were lying! Let me do it, yer too fucking slow!" He then pushed her with such force, she felt herself losing balance, catching herself badly on the chair arm as she hit the floor. She felt her hip crack, the

40

pain was unbearable. She watched as he searched the wardrobe, throwing things angrily, two boxes hit her as she lay there, unable to move.

He turned triumphant, clutching a bundle of notes. "Yeh! This is what I'm looking for...not a lot for yer life's savings Granma, is it? Not as if you've spent much on yer 'ouse, or yersel'. Yer not trying t'trick me are yer, 'ave yer got some hidden somewhere else?" As he stuffs the notes into his pocket, he steps towards her, standing over her with a vile look on his face.

"I have no other savings...please believe me. I've lent money to my daughter. The grandsons needed a car... please....please don't hurt me..." He leaned over her, his face coming towards hers. She could smell the stench of onions and cigarette smoke on his breath. "The fuckin' grandsons needed a car..." He mocked. "Spose they'll have a nice posh motor then, 'spose they've got nice posh jobs an all."

41

Doris was now feeling faint with the pain.

If she talked to him, maybe she could calm him down. "They're at university, working hard, it's not a 'posh' car, it's just a second-hand car...have you got a job, you could get a nice car... maybe...."

"Shut yer yap Granma! Why would I need a job? I get paid t'do fuck all...extra dosh ont side from thieving. Fuckin' mugs game gettin' a job." He swaggered back smugly.

Doris tried her best to move, the pain was shifting through her body.   "Please...could you help me up, the pain, please...don't leave me on the floor." Before Doris could take her next breath, he grabbed hold of her bruised, swollen arm, he'd hit earlier, pulling her whole body upwards, he swung her tiny frame like a ragdoll, onto the bed. She could feel herself almost passing out as she landed on her damaged hip.

She cried out. "Oh, Arthur save me! Oh, dear God, please save me..."

The pain made her gasp in agony. As he let go, he stood there, at the end of the bed ...should he? He began to feel that urge again......He'd had an oldie before....

Doris couldn't move, she felt him grabbing at her night-gown...she prayed for release....she prayed for death to take her, rather than this animal ...she prayed for Arthur to save her...she prayed to God to forgive her for whatever she'd done to deserve this...she just prayed and prayed......and prayed..........

Her eyes now streaming with tears, she felt the searing pain crescendo ...she felt urine flowing from her wrecked body, as the fear engulfed her, with a desperate last gasp for air she slipped into unconsciousness....

Dabber stood for several minutes, finally moving away from the thin, wrinkly body, how could he be that desperate. How old did you have to be, to be that revolting to look at.... His gran was a fit looking bird of forty-six. This must be bloody ancient, should have been in one of them homes out the way. He was doing everyone a favour, one less, no loss.

He began laughing to himself as he searched the rest of the bedroom and the remaining rooms. Not much of a haul, bit of jewellery, two rings from her fingers, couple of men's rings on the dressing table. He tried on the square stoned one, bit o' bling for himself. He'd take the rest to Mad Phil, he'd give a fair price, or trade.

He kicked Monty's lifeless body as he passed on the landing. He went downstairs to continue his search. A few more quid in her handbag, bit in a tea-caddy in the kitchen ...same old places, as he sneered to himself in smug triumph. He took the cheque book and card. He'd sell them onto Liz Feenan. She did all that cheque and card fraud, he couldn't be arsed   with all that.

Nice watch in the top desk drawer, he saw the engraved initials and put it back, easy to ID, he'd made that mistake before. He went back into the kitchen, opening the fridge door, helping himself to a drink of milk. Straight from the carton, he wouldn't be leaving any glasses for the pigs to check for his....DNR? Summut' like that. All he knew was that they could pin the lot on yer if they found it.

He unlocked the back door, sniggering to himself as he saw all the locks and bolts. He was feeling fuckin' great, another burglary well done, life was good.

He stopped, momentarily at the front gate, then walked quickly up the road hoping he was going in the right direction for Kieron's, finally seeing a road he recognised. He back tracked, taking the second turning off, now knowing he was in Central Avenue.

The Parkers stayed up all hours. Sure enough, the lights were on, people were

45

in, the door left ajar, a sign from Kieron and Shell that they were still open for business.

Dabber pushed his way through, past a young lad leaving with a couple of carrier bags full, on into the front room.

"Yo, Kizzer mate, how's it hanging?" Kieron looked up, his glazed eyes trying to focus. "Yay!...Dabber....mate...where yer bin....'ere, 'ave a bottle." He sways backwards slightly, reaching into a box behind the huge, cream leather sofa.

"Jojo and Finn did that cash n' carry job, I got a few supplies in." He grins drunkenly and waves a bottle of vodka at Dabber. "I'll let yer 'ave it for a fiver mate."

Dabber reaches into his pocket, pulling out a wad of notes. "I'll take two for now mate, I may get someone to share the other one with later." He takes a sly look at Shell and winks. She in turn, leans forward to flick her cigarette in the large, free standing, onyx ashtray, knowing full well she's giving Dabber an eyeful of her ample cleavage.

The two customers in the corner of the room finish sorting through the goods on the table and pass Shell some cash. Stolen booze, cigarettes, and a couple of designer tops, she acquired in her day job......shoplifting. They leave saying they'll be back Friday night, see what she's got in then.

"Ave yer come for a bender Dabber, mate? Finn's gone to doss at Jojo's, now he's working for Milo. There's a room free if Earl's pissin' yer off like?"

Kieron then starts to wave his arms like a deranged Kermit the frog, the substances now reaching what little he has left for a brain. "Help yersel man, yer know yer always welcome 'ere... Shell, where's me sarnie, babe...I'm starvin'." He then flops back into his chair in a semi-comatose state.

Shell stands up slowly, bending low again to stub her cigarette out, giving Dabber another eyeful of what's for dessert, if he's lucky. She stands in front of Kieron, who's head is beginning to loll sideways. She then turns herself round, so that she is between the two, but facing Dabber.

"Do you fancy a quick sandwich Dwayne? I quite fancy something with a bit of meat in it me'sel, what d'ya say?"

Dabber feels his groin ache. Another ten, fifteen minutes at the most and Kieron would be asleep, then he'd get her over that kitchen counter and give her all the meat she needed, the horny bitch. "I'll just have a drink with me old mucker, Shell, then I'll be in there, t' see just what you've got….eh babe?" He glances quickly at Kieron, then winks at her, before she disappears.

He's now finding it difficult to think of anything to say, with his mind on what was possibly waiting for him in the kitchen. Fortunately, Kizzer is well blitzed.

"Dya' wont another drink mate?" Dabber nudged him and prodded him quite hard, just to make sure. Thank fuck for that, he was well gone.

He quickly headed to the kitchen. He was finally going to get something tasty for supper.

Chapter 4

Stretching his arms up behind his head, Harry Robinson yawned loudly...

"Come on, get yourself out of bed!" Telling himself off, for the final time as he turns his head towards the clock. He's clicked the snooze button twice now. He's had a good eight hours, not bad for him. Rubbing his face, he makes his way downstairs, clicking the kettle on as he wanders through the kitchen to the bathroom, climbs into the shower, his big frame taking up most of the cubicle.

Fifteen minutes later he prizes a set of overalls out of the laundry basket. "Sorry mum." He says, looking skywards. He'd not had time to iron them, but at least they were clean.

That's what used to keep his old mum going, endless washing and ironing. The Doctors were amazed how she kept going, pottering on, cleaning and cooking. They'd given her six months. She'd seen out an extra year. She'd told Dr Phillips she couldn't leave her son Harry and cat, Billy, as they wouldn't manage without her.

But her illness had been the last straw for Harry's fiancée, she'd left him when he moved back with his old mum. He'd felt guilty on both counts.

His dad had died when he was sixteen, he'd skipped school, not done as well as he should. Maybe he'd contributed to his mum's poor health. It took her years to get over losing dad and he hadn't exactly been the caring, attentive son he could have been.

He and mum should have supported each other more, instead he resented being stuck at home, while his sister, Fern, went off to college, met and married Tim and moved away. He started going out late, coming home all hours, but eventually began to feel more settled when he met Jilly and moved into her little flat in Linthorpe village.

He began to pop in to see mum again. Uncle Nat got him the job at the Florence Street depot, just across town. He and mum really started to enjoy each other's company. She'd started baking again and would wrap loads of cakes and pies up for him. Of course, Jilly saw it as a slight, a criticism of her cooking. Although he had to admit M&S prawn balls in oyster sauce with wild rice ready meals weren't exactly cooking and certainly no match for his mum's steak and kidney pies.

Mum tried to brush off the Doctors findings to Harry when he insisted on moving back and had finally found out just how ill she was. He felt he wanted to make whatever time she had left enjoyable and comfortable. He wanted her to feel as important and as loved, as she had made him feel as a boy.

Jilly didn't understand, she wasn't really a family person. She'd moved away from home at seventeen, rarely rang her parents, never wanted children. In fact sometimes he wondered how they got together. He remembers, he was trying to ask her friend out, the night they'd met, but Jilly had been determined to push her 'friend' out and bag Harry for herself. He was flattered by her continued attention, she arranged everything, he just went along with it all, until two years ago when he decided to move back with mum, just while she was ill. Jilly didn't understand that, to be honest she didn't want to. She'd never called or been in touch since.

Then mum died and.........and well, he'd been alone ever since.

Lucky escape I suppose. Thanks mum. He smiles upwards again, quickly fussing and feeding Billy with one hand, gulping down a cup of tea and grabbing a slice of toast with the other. Keys, coat, rucksack, and he was off.

He steers dad's old bike carefully down the hall passage and out into the morning sun. He peddles off down Essex Street, picks up speed into Parliament Road, down Union Street, tutting at all the litter. 'Why do people buy kebabs if they're only going throw half of it away? Messy blighters!' He weaves his way on through the town, between the cars and buses.

He never took his driving test, never saw the point. Cycled everywhere, always had. He and his dad used to cycle miles when he was a boy. They'd go all the way out into the countryside, to Great Ayton where Captain Cook went to school. History didn't seem so boring when his dad told him stuff. They'd stop in the village for an ice-cream. To a ten-year-old boy from the town, the place seemed like the back of beyond.

They'd cycle all the way to Preston Park. They'd take a packed lunch and sit by the river. His dad would tell him all about his duties in the war, his buddies who'd lost their lives, he'd listened in awe. His dad was his hero. They were all heroes.

He was saddened for those wonderful, brave souls, who were now, 'the elderly'. Fearful and totally lost in a world they fought for. When they were all young, spirited, and optimistic for a world of peace, fairness, and good fortune. That world was long gone, left was a world of crime, violence, religious hatred, terrorism, and fear. This country was full to the brim with, thieving, lazy scum, all wanting, something for nothing. Sitting on their backsides, waiting for the state to pay up, no one seemed to take responsibility for themselves, or their kids anymore. It's always someone else's fault.

55

Harry despised the way the elderly was treated, who'd been through so much and paid their way. Always bottom of the list, poor pensions, ignored in hospitals, pen-pushers at the top just seeing them as a waste of money. The government grasping inheritance tax, anything they can squeeze out of their   hard-earned savings. Poor souls who think they've done the right thing by working hard and saving and wanting to keep their independence. Living in houses the government and councils and greedy builders want them out of so they can make money by turning them into flats or knocking them down. By now Harry's anger is rising, his frustration coming out in his cycling, as he peddles like the wind onto North Road, taking a fast corner into Lloyd Street.

"Eh! Harry! Watch it mate, where's the fire, you nearly took me toes off!"

"Oh! Sorry Mal, thought I was running late." Malcolm takes a step back to protect his feet. "Running late, peddling that fast you could be going for the land speed record! Ken's just got into the office, yer fine mate. Mek us a brew, I'll just check the wagon."

Harry quickly makes a row of teas and swaps his coat for his hi-vis jacket, he then perches on the edge of the large old chair in the corner and takes a sip from a strong, much needed cuppa. He hears Ken's voice and quickly puts the mug down, stands up and begins zipping up his jacket.

"Don't look so guilty Harry, Norm's not in yet. Finish yer brew mate, fine by me as long as you're out by eight. Hey and try not to add anymore old'uns to that list of yours." Harry looks startled. "What...what do yer mean?"

Ken laughs and pats his shoulder. "Mal's been telling me. Apparently, you're the old'uns friend, telling them not to drag their bins to the front. Leave the gate unlatched, on pick up day and you'll take tod bin out for them?"

"Ah, sorry Ken, but some of those bags and bins are so heavy, my old mum always had a struggle, it's not fair to expect them to…….."

Ken raises his hands in mock defeat. "Hey Harry, I'm not havin' a go mate. You're a good bloke, sound as a pound. I know how you feel about the way the old'uns are treated... I'm just saying, no more on your list, I can't afford to pay you extra time for doing yer bit for 'Help The Aged'."

Harry knew exactly what Ken meant, he couldn't really expect his principles to be added on as overtime. "No more on the list Ken...but what if I jog the round instead of walking...?" He knew by Ken's expression he was pushing his luck. Ken was a good boss and a fair man.

"You do and you'll be jogging off into the sunset with yer P45, so think on." Ken left, shaking his head, but quietly amused. Harry was a bloke in a million, heart of gold, strength of a lion and as soft as clart.

By eight thirty the refuse wagon had just turned off Acklam Road. "I'll take odds down Maldon Road Mal, you and Jeff can take evens, okay?" Harry gave the orders as he slid from his wagon seat and onto the pavement.

Mal grinned, "Yeah, as long as we get a share of the cake and biscuits from all yer adoptive grannies, eh Jeff?"

"I just promised I'd change the bulb in Mrs Linton's outside light, I won't be long, honest." Barry put the thumbs up as he drove off slowly.

"We'll get the odds on our way back up, you're alright for ten mate."

Harry swung the unlatched gate open and went towards the back door. Even though he could see it was open a little, he was polite enough to know to knock and wait till Doris came to it, rather than just barge in. He waited a minute or two, then pushed the door with one finger. "Mrs Linton... Mrs Linton! It's Harry, I've just come to change the bulb ...you know, for the outside light."

He waited, then peered into the kitchen, the switch for the outside light was just there, on the inside wall. Maybe she was still getting dressed, or in the bath, his mother had always preferred a morning soak.

"Mrs Linton!" Harry called out again. "It's ok, I can just change the bulb, take the rubbish, if you're busy, it's not a problem, no need to rush yourself."

He reached in and clicked the outdoor light switch, the bulb flashed on. Harry looked puzzled. It was working. The bulb was fine. Maybe Doris was becoming a bit confused, or maybe she just needed the excuse for a bit of company.

He began to feel guilty again, guilty for his mum, for Doris...for all the Doris Linton's, that had no daily company, no one close they could trust, no one there when they needed them. He'd wait till she appeared, have a quick chat, accept her cake and biscuits, just whatever made her day.

He stepped inside, just about to call out again when he noticed the ornamental tea caddy that Doris had told him came from her Great Aunt Lily. It was down from the shelf, with the lid off. He had no idea what it had contained, but he began to feel a little uneasy. Doris was normally up with the lark unless her back was playing up. Maybe she was ill, had medication been in the tea-caddy, maybe she's fallen somewhere... He stepped into the hall, glancing through the lounge door.

"Mrs Linton, ...Doris... Doris! Are you alright?"
He noticed a picture on the carpet of the lounge, the desk drawer pulled open, he began to feel the hairs on the back of his neck prickling, he had nauseous tight feeling welling in his stomach as he reached the bottom of the stairs and looked upwards. Arms and head outstretched from the landing over the top stair, eyes still open, lay the body of Doris's cat, Monty, bloodied and lifeless.

Panic took over, Harry began to shout. "Mrs Linton! Are you alright? Look, I'm sorry if you're in the bath, getting dressed, whatever, I need to know you're okay, I need to know you're..." He charged up the stairs like a rhino, two at a time, spare bedroom, bathroom then Doris and Arthur's room.

"I need to know you're not......" He stopped abruptly, stock still, staring in disbelief, his hand went to his mouth as he felt bile rising and nausea taking hold, hardly daring to a breath, his eyes took in the degrading and shameful sight.

Doris lay there, prostrate across the bed, with its pretty old-fashioned, rosebud covered bed sheets. Her arm and hand were set towards the bedside table, towards the telephone. Her tissue paper thin skin, multi-coloured, in large areas of bruising. The dark savage purple showing up starkly against her paleness.

Both her and her late husband's belongings and precious mementos of their life together strewn all over the room, spilling out of opened cupboards and drawers. Boxes had even been thrown on top of her, as if she were no longer human, just part of the contents of the room.

Harry's eyes welled with tears of anger, tears of hurt, imagining this poor frightened, defenceless soul, her last minutes on earth were spent facing the scum that did this to her. He gently moved the boxes. He checked her pulse, gently rubbing her

63

hand with his huge fingers, in the hope of signs of life and talking softly to her, just in case she could still hear him.

Realising the awful truth, he reaches for the phone and calls the police. He knew they'd soon be here, but just to save, Mrs Doris Linton, a last modicum of dignity, he pulls down her pale lilac night-gown from under her chin to cover up her body. Nobody.......nobody, should die like this and nobody should be found like this.

Before he leaves the room Harry again gently touches her hand. Almost unable to speak, he whispers through his tears. "I am so, so sorry Doris, I hope your Arthur came for you and saved you from the worst. I promise I will do my utmost to get the person, or people who did this to you ...for both of you... God bless."

Chapter 5

Detective Inspector Hayman strides through to the main CID office checking the number of officers in the room. "We've got a suspicious death on Maldon Road, elderly female. I need a DS and two DC's with me at the scene. Kenny, have you got two of your team available?"

"Well, Fuller is in sir, Felling and Scott should be on their way but..."

"My team are in sir, I can bring Ambrose and Chapman with me, Peel and Grant can organise the Incident room sir." Beth mouthed her apologies towards Kenny, as she grabbed her jacket. Kenny shrugged in accepting defeat.

"Not to worry, maybe I'll get a charming suspect to interview? You jumped in there a bit quick, money worries, hoping for a runner?"

"Sort of, Mum and Dad have had a crappy couple of years. I've booked a nice break for them, I wanted all the trimmings, I think it's going to cost a little more than I thought. Any overtime is better than none...…but get your thumb screws ready, I'll try and bring you one of our towns finest to torture. See you later." She grabbed some keys off the board, tall and athletic, she was down in the back yard and jumping into the car in minutes.

DC Chapman and Ambrose climb into the car, looking a little less fit and enthusiastic. Beth tuts and takes off out the yard as they've barely closed the doors.

"Chappy, are SOCO there yet, have we got enough kit in the boot and are you two awake enough to cope?"

"Yes, to all three." DC Chapman states calmly. "Hey, I've just heard old 'Wahay' talking to SOCO on the radio. 'Come in SOCO Humphries, we're just approaching the West Lane junction, we're about to... drive, drive, drive!' What is he on? He was born too late, should have been flying Spitfires."

"It's that moustache, it's taking him over...." Pud adds, laughing.

"Will you two pack it in, let's start to focus shall we, suspicious death, elderly female...Maldon Road"

"Oh, get her! Sorry, all powerful one, zone, centre, focus. Not sure 1 can, already did that on the bog this morning, I'm all centred out..."

"Yes, thank you boys, I realise the adrenaline is pumping........don't even think it." She wags her finger at Chappie, then can't help but laugh at his expression.

It wasn't that they were callous, or blasé about the situation they were about to deal with, or the scene they were about to walk into, it was just the opposite. Deep down inside, they knew they *had* to deal with it. It's what the public expects of them.   Robotic neutrality.

Police are presumed to be not quite like everyone else. Standard procedures to follow, no emotion allowed, no opinions, unless of stated fact and hard evidence. Even colleagues keep up the show. Emotion is for wimps. Show it and you become a weak link. Nothing more than resilience and strength of character can be seen.

Probably why so many of them find, 'outside pursuits' to relieve such inhuman stress. Drinking, affairs, gambling, or of course, like herself, an ironically, 'unhealthy' pursuit of the gym and obsessive exercise regimes. You just *have* to channel that stress and anger. To deal with, day in and day out, the endless lack of justice, the unfair media snipes at the force, the constant finger pointing and inhouse squabbling. The hundred weight of paperwork, the lack of praise when something goes right, but the ritual slaughter and 'right royal bollocking' and example making, when something goes wrong.

Beth sighed deeply as she turned into Maldon Road. "Come on boys, let's get this circus up and running." As they walked towards the crime scene tape, with PC Morrison at the gate, Beth felt her hackles rise as she turned to see the 'rubber-neckers' and the ghouls of the parish arriving.

"Can you make sure the road is closed off a bit further down Glen, obviously word has got out already, judging by all the local interest. I presume these are all friends and neighbours of the deceased…Not! Who no doubt, will be putting their bunch of flowers out front when there's a news camera here and giving their   two-penneth about how awful this is, she was such a lovely person......Yeh! So lovely they never bothered to call and give her flowers when she was alive, or ask if she needed anything, or show any concern until there's a local TV reporter stuffing a microphone into their egotistical little faces!"

She mentally counted to ten while putting the rather awkward paper suit on and ludicrous looking over shoes. Typical she'd put a skirt on today, it felt like she was wearing an uncomfortable pair of culottes.

An angry male in a navy tracksuit came striding towards the barrier.

"Where were the pigs when the old girl was murdered eh? Bloody typical, some mad, murdering bastard walking the streets, but never any bloody cops about when yer need em'!" The usual ringleaders begin to chant. With gritted teeth Beth and her men head towards the back door.

DI Hayman, having already been there ten minutes had assessed the scene. He strides back towards Beth, through the kitchen.

"SOCO working their way through, photographs have been taken. Body still in situ, I think you should take a look soon as Beth. The men in black are on their way. Body is believed to be that of an.... elderly, white female. We assume, Doris Linton, aged 82years, ascertained from documents found. Believed widowed and living alone. Doctor's in, he's pronounced life extinct. This is a bad one Beth, this is not going to be easy. Just got to hope there's some prints somewhere, we could do with catching this bastard quickly, for everyone's sake."

All three Detectives squeezed past the DI who is now on his radio, requesting the incident room at headquarters to be opened. "At least ten on it, get an analyst on standby and can I have another four PC's for out front, the hyenas are circling, get my drift Tom?"

Beth hears a voice from upstairs. "Is that DS Flynn down there? Are you going to take a look first before I begin taking samples and dusting?"

"Is that Terry H, SOCO extraordinaire? Hunter by name, hunter by nature?"

Beth climbs the stairs listening for which room his voice is coming from. "Sorry, this isn't pleasanter circumstances. I'll tell you Beth, if there is ever a slim chance, they decide to bring back capital punishment, I'd happily administer the lethal dose myself on this one. The poor soul ending her days like this."

Beth steels herself, as she steps carefully past the body, of a large black and white cat, she looks from its congealed fur to the blood spattered up the landing wall. Old ladies and cats, this was one cowardly piece of shit they were looking for.

DC Pud Ambrose swore under his breath, as he and Chappie followed Beth into the bedroom and an unholy crime scene. It was his first real body in situ, it was a hell of a lot different to a dummy in a training scene. He'd only been with CID two months. He'd seen assaults, RTAs, he'd even been to a post-mortem during training, but it didn't prepare you for this. He felt a little queasy and swallowed hard.

"Pud, could you do me a favour, can you just get me a couple of extra pairs of gloves from the boot and my little torch, I think I left it on the dash, thanks."

Beth had seen his changing colour and knew a couple of minutes in the fresh air would get him sorted. No need to make a fuss.

She remembered being sick in an empty evidence bag on *her* first serious crime scene, nearly ten years ago now. But if she was honest, it didn't get any easier. With every serious crime she dealt with, it just made her more determined to catch whoever did it. Sadly, the justice handed out to the criminals, after they'd done the catching, was a different story altogether.

With Chappie close behind, they took in the scene, carefully recording every tiny detail. Every inch, every possession, item of clothing, every wound, every stain, trying to piece together the last terrifying minutes of this frail human being's life.

Beth looked over at the Doctor standing by the window, writing up his notes. "Can you give us a cause of death, approximate time, Doctor Collins?" His eyes peered at her, over the rim of his specs.

"Mmm...difficult to say. She has extensive bruising, start of partial rigor, the wrist set looks broken, possibly even the right hip as well, judging by the leg position and colour. There are no signs of marks to the neck, or mouth, no blue tinge to the lips, no raise to the temperature. Obviously, I can't rule it out, but it doesn't appear to be asphyxia. Hard to say, she obviously suffered severe trauma and death was probably between 10pm and 1am. Needless to say, there appears to be little or no struggle, although the wrist could be a defence wound."

Beth gritted her teeth and took a deep breath.

"Was she......sexually assaulted, Doctor?" Doctor Collins slid the night-gown up slightly, showing obvious finger mark bruising on the inner left leg above the knee. "I really can't tell you from what I've seen, you'll need the PM and forensics to tell you that for certain, but I think sadly, it maybe a distinct possibility."

"Perverted, sadistic bastard! Bad enough he scares the living daylights out of her, inflicting pain on a defenceless old lady, but raping her...the sick piece of shit." DC Chapman clenches his fists to release the anger.

"God...this could be my mother, my gran. What will the lowlife get when he's caught, life in prison? Huh! Don't make me laugh. Three free meals a day, no debts, education, if you can be bothered, movies, a gym, counselling, bloody art classes! It's laughable if it weren't so sick! Sling them all on a disused oil rig in the middle of the ocean, with a couple of sacks of porridge dropped in once a bloody month. Who'd miss 'em, bastards?" Chappie turned away angry at himself for his opinionated outburst.

"Why waste the porridge? Make them do something useful for once in their squalid, horrid little lives. Two choices, the lethal injection, or to be used in medical experimentation? They take a life why should they not accept they have to give up theirs. Give them that choice. The victims don't get a choice, why should the perpetrator get a choice."

Everyone looks over at Doctor Collins, he begins to feel a little awkward. "Yes, I know, I know, a tad controversial perhaps, but worth a thought, they're very short of cadavers at medical schools."

Beth then went on to save yet another male, from a potentially embarrassing situation. "Well, before we put him on an oil rig and dissect him, in the interests of medical science we'd better find the revolting excuse for a human being first. Right lads?"

The Doctor clicked shut his case and stepped from the room just as Pud came back with at least twenty pairs of gloves." Beth smiled. "I know we women are supposed to be able to multitask Pud, but I'm not an octopus."

As the officers look through cupboards and drawers, Beth pulls on her gloves and moves slowly and carefully stepping over the items on the floor. She then picks up two photographs from the bedside table. One shows a handsome young man in uniform, with a dainty young girl gazing up at him. In the other, the features were still there, many years on, but they had that same look in their eyes. All those years later still that look of love and respect.

Beth wished she'd seen that look in Mark's eyes, seven years ago, then

78

maybe she wouldn't have been divorced four years later. What was it that kept people married for forty, fifty years or more? Honesty, morality, loyalty, respect?

Beth put the photos back carefully and crouched down by the bedside. She gazed over the pale extinguished body, the shell of what was left of the beautiful girl in the photo. She ran her fingers gently over the dreadful discoloured, bruised skin. She'd seen it all before.

It wasn't the scene that got to her, so much as what had led up to it. How terrified would this poor lady have been? ...The total indignity of such a vile attack.

Beth whispered under her breath, "He won't get away with it, not this time."

"Who won't?" SOCO Hunter strides towards her, cases full of equipment. "Oh ...you know what it's like Terry. The person who did this, they'll have built up to it. Indecent exposure, female muggings perhaps, indecent assaults even. We'll have a record of something, somewhere...hopefully. I'll start going through some files back at the office before the PM. Meanwhile, my 'bestest' SOCO expert will find all sorts of clues, samples and hopefully prints, won't he?" She looks at him expectantly.

Terry smiles. "You know me Beth, flattery will get you everywhere...and that is where me ali powder will be going in a minute, so if you don't want a silver face, I suggest you leave me to it. I'll let you know what I find?"

"Right you are then. Don't forget the phone by the bed just in case he took it out of her hand. Some fibres would be great and pack up all the bedding. Oh, and don't forget to cover and bag the hands and take that jewellery box for the glue cabinet and....." Terry narrowed his eyes and starts twizzling his powder brush threateningly. "You wouldn't just like to come and do my job for me would you?"

"And end up looking like a demented Cyberman, no I would not! I'll make sure we get some tea sent up for you. Just do your best Terry, it means a lot to me on this one and I don't mean another pip on the shoulder of me uniform either."

She catches Chappie and Pud as they're leaving the room. "Can you two just check the other rooms. See if you can find details of a next of kin and one of you get on the radio, see if we've got enough officers on their way to start house to house enquiries."

Beth carefully makes her way through the team of forensic experts and out into the glaring sunlight and breaths in deeply. "Who found her PC Morrison?"

He flicks through his pocketbook and sheets on his clipboard. "Errm, that would be a, Harold Peter Robinson, known as Harry. Refuse collector, he found the deceased at approximately 8.35am, call came through to the switchboard at 8.48am   Sarge."

"What was he doing in her house, did he know her? Where is Mr Robinson now Glen? Is that him over there, by the wagon?" Beth begins to walk towards Mal and Jeff, who are both looking pale and worried.

"No, DS Flynn, he's there, with the paramedic, they think he's suffering from shock." PC Morrison points towards the ambulance.

"Mr Robinson, Harold Robinson? How are you feeling? This must be an awful shock for you. I realise this may be difficult at this time, but could I just ask you a couple of questions? Why were...."

Beth turns quickly as she hears Chappie shouting. "Sarge! Sarge...quick, there's someone still in the house! The spare bedroom, hiding in the wardrobe, we'll wait for you. It's your shout!" Beth sees Chappie disappear back into the house, she's up and running, the adrenaline pumping through her body.

"Let me go!......I want to get the bastard first!"
Two paramedics have trouble holding Harry back, his
anger rising again. "I'll kill him!"

A couple of the crowd hear the commotion. The
chanting begin again, like baying hounds waiting to rip
apart their pray. Not if I get there first thought Beth,
cursing under her breath as she charges up the stairs.

"Have you seen him? Big, small, do we know
him, …what?" Chappie looks at Pud and back to Beth.

Pud answers quietly. "Err...no Sarge, I just heard
a noise in the wardrobe, I was checking the drawers so I
just rushed out and held the door shut, he can't escape,
window has a lock on..."

Beth knew she looked ridiculous in the paper suit,
but she had her stat body armour on. It was an opportunity
she wasn't going to back out of. "Have you got a baton
handy?" She held out a hand towards Chappie. Grabbing

83

it, she swished it hard, it extended fully, she steadied her nerve. "Right Pud, hold that door handle, when I say, 'now' push it open, as quick as you can, stand back and two of you come in behind me, cuffs ready, okay?" They all nodded. "Okay Sarge."

"Now! Go, go, go!"

Beth rushes through the open door almost colliding with the far wall the room was so small, but no one there. She turns in seconds towards the wardrobe doors, she could hear rustling coming from inside. Her heart pounding, she quietly signalled for Chappie to open the right side the same time she opened the left, she had the baton raised in her right hand. "Police! We're going to open the wardrobe door. We want you to stay still, do not move until we say so. Stay still! Doors opening... now!"

The doors flung open, everything and everyone went quiet as they took in the sight, from on top of a pile of brown paper, blankets and old hats, a pair of frightened eyes peered out at them.

"It's a bloody cat...you silly sod…......It's a bloody cat…you nuggit!"

Chappie turned to Pud with obvious relief.

"Look at the poor little bugger, it's bloody terrified." Pud looked from the cat to Chappie, who carefully lifted Tibby from the wardrobe as it clung on to a small blue hat. "Yeh, you'd be terrified seeing daylight and four shouting faces looming over you while you're trying to bed down in a wardrobe for a kip."

DC Chapman sent a PC to get a box to put the cat in. "Well, it can't stay here it might contaminate the scene." He says in his defence, as he catches Beth's raised eyebrows and her heart stops pounding.

Then Chappie, realising a more suitable excuse says. "Having said that, we'd better take a sample of hair, from both cats, in case we get a suspect in."

Tibby began to purr quietly as Chappie automatically began to stroke the frightened animal as he spoke. "Well, you big softie DC Chapman. Never knew you were a cat lover."

"Neither did I, till me girlfriend left me 10 months ago, with three of them! She left them too, but not for the same reasons, she didn't think they'd be too keen on Dog Handler PC Callahan's two great big German Shepherds. I just wasn't too keen on PC Callahan, if you get me drift?"

"Oh, sorry Chappie, just you and the cats then now is it? How sweet." Said Beth smiling.

"Yep, just me and the boys now, Harpo, Groucho and Zeppo, you're more than welcome to pop round. One of our favourite evenings is settling down to milk, prawn cocktail crisps and a couple of DVDs...usually 'Finding Nemo', or 'Jaws' depending on our moods and what sort of day we've had."

Beth began to laugh, her adrenaline rush now subsiding. "Sorry, don't think your boys would appreciate my Jack Russell, Freddie. We're more a four-mile jog, then home to lemon tea and salad and relax with a book, crime novel, or biography .... depending on *our* day!"

"Apparently it's very therapeutic, stroking cats, very beneficial to lowering stress levels." DC Chapman says, raising his eyebrows.

"So is a session of kick boxing, followed by thirty minutes of Yoga."

Chappie looks worn out at the very thought and heads towards the door.

Clutching his cat box, he feigns a dejected expression. "Hey, me and me moggies know when we're not wanted, we'll just go back to pummelling cushions and batting toy mice up and down the hall, don't you worry about us."

Beth grabs hold of his belt tucking his baton carefully back into its pouch. "Me and Freddie are not averse to a bit of cushion pummelling ...but our bone chewing can put off many a visitor, it's not a pretty sight... grrrrr."

Beth laughs, as Chappie retorts quickly. "If I can get to the butchers before closing time, which do you prefer, lamb or beef?"

He never stopped. There was nothing in it, just stress releasing banter.

Police officers are charmers by nature, they have to be. How on earth would you get anyone to open-up in interview otherwise and tell you what you need to know, to give information, to feel trust, feel they cared about what happens to you and want to know why you do what you do, your reasons, your opinions.

Part of Police training. Cognitive interview techniques. The long pauses after a question, endless patience, the eye contact, listening intently to what they have to say. People admire their politeness, consideration, and attentiveness. With a witness it gets information and evidence, but more importantly, from a suspect, eventual confession hopefully.

With the public it gets them trust and respect by the majority. On the opposite sex, very often, devotion and ultimately anything they want with no questions asked. But not everyone feels the same, some just feel plain and simply duped.

Beth had had her fingers burnt on occasion throughout her career with the force. She had vowed, harmless flirting and humorous banter was as far as it would go. She would accept dates, but preferably not from police officers...Scenes of Crime officers...or pathologists, (her ex-husbands profession). Probably why she was still home alone with the dog after an average 10-hour shift, spending far too much time at the gym and visiting her parents every other weekend.

She rallied herself back into focus as an officer from Kenny's shift walked towards her. "We've been given the action to go and speak to the next of kin Beth, do you want to come with us? They live at York. Doris Linton has one daughter Henrietta, husband Russell, surname of Beech. They have twin sons, James and Daniel. Kenny reckons you'll be better with the daughter and family."

She didn't want this action any more than Kenny but knew she would be the better choice to break the news to them. Kenny would be matter of fact and unresponsive to their emotions, most likely push Family Liason in first,

so he could leave them to, 'mop up' as he put it.

Chapter 6

Over three hours later, they finally got back from

York and into the station,

they'd barely spoken. As soon they got back into the building, heading towards the office, Beth left the lads in the corridor and headed toward the ladies toilets. Grabbing a cubicle, sitting down heavily on the toilet lid, she felt the tears break and stream from her eyes, she bit her lip hard so that she wouldn't make a sound. She was no weak link and wasn't about to let anyone consider otherwise. But she was human.

Henrietta Beech had opened the door to them, a lovely warm, gentle woman. No doubt, very much her mother's daughter. Within minutes of them speaking she was a weak and sobbing wreck, her eyes pleading for them to tell her it wasn't true. Russell, her husband, on being called at work, was home within twenty minutes, holding her close, trying to be strong, his eyes welling with tears, the shock of the details beyond comprehension.

As their good neighbour, Aggie Marsh, had been called in by one of the officers, she quietly and stoically made tea, the twins returned home from a friend's house round the corner. Tears turned to anger for the boys, they were all for driving up to Middlesbrough and hunting the culprit down.

Henrietta's shock quickly turned to guilt. She should have got herself in gear, she should have sorted it out for mum to move in with them, they should have put her first for once, she always, put them first.

Beth and Kenny's DCs Fuller and Scott, got the details they needed then tried their hardest to reassure the Beech family that they were doing everything they could to catch the person who did this to Doris...... their mother...... their grandmother. They would keep them informed every step of the way. Family Liaison and Victim Support had been informed and would be with them shortly. It all felt such a totally inadequate statement, watching this family cling together in such heartache, such unnecessary pain.

Beth closed her eyes tightly, gritted her teeth, she knew what she had to do. Real justice had to be served here, the person who could commit these sorts of crimes was the lowest of the low, cruel, desperate, perverted and vile, he had to be stopped. She took a deep breath, unlocked the cubicle door, splashed her face with cold water, re-applied her lipstick, held her head up and walked purposefully back to the office.

"Wondered where you'd got to, are you okay?" Chappie walked towards her trying to catch her eye. "Call of nature, far too much of Aggie's tea, what did you get me for our very late lunch then?" She smiled making notes with one hand, clicking her computer to life with the other.

"Your favourite madam, ham salad in granary....no mayo, the perfect, combination of wholegrain, carbohydrates, protein and minerals...." He raises an eyebrow.

"Yes, Chappie thank you, anyone would think I was some sort of health junkie, it's just common sense, that's all. I hope you remembered my fresh orange too?" She grinned as he carefully placed the straw in the carton and went back to his own 'healthy' delights of a sausage and egg bun and large milky coffee with three sugars.

She looked at her list of contacts. She tapped in the SOCO extension on her phone. "Terry, what have you got?" She grabbed her pen and began scribbling down anything of significance.

"Well, as you can imagine, there are numerous fingerprint lifts to be checked. WPC Taylor is just bringing in the family's elim prints from York, PC Riaz has just got the binman, Robinson's elims after he gave his witness statement. The house-to-house officers are checking with the neighbours, as to who else may have had access to Mrs. Linton's home. Obviously, we're awaiting the post-mortem results as well." He heard a muttered curse, then a drawer slam shut.

"Oh! Sorry Terry, I'm supposed to be at the post-mortem at four, the DI will kill me!" Terry chuckles, "I think one dead body at a time is enough, even for him. Speak to you later."

"Chappie, finish yer bun on the way, I'll drive." He's looking puzzled and just licking the dribbled egg yolk from his tie.

She raises her arms in despair. "The post-mortem! We're supposed to be there...now!" He sighs, taking a large gulp of sweet frothy coffee.

"Just as well I've got a full stomach then, nothing worse than hoying up bile, tastes worse than your healthy so-called sandwich, but only just!"

"Yes, thank you Doctor Chapman, I think we've got the picture, you with your head in the sluice room sink, isn't one of my favourites!"

Fifteen minutes later they're ringing the bell of the mortuary, but never without Chappie going into his Bela Lugosi impression and trying not to snigger, as the door creaks open. They so wanted Lurch to be there saying, 'yooouu raaaang'! Puerile stuff, but it's what keeps them going in such awful places and circumstances. The cold of the mortuary fridges hits them as they walk in.

Katy Irish was the last person you would expect to see working in a mortuary. She was small and elfin with sharp features and large, brown, happy eyes. The medical clothes drown her, the white wellies up to her knees the plastic apron, rolled and tied so it didn't hit the floor. She was bright and cheerful, but also efficient and caring, always considerate and compassionate with relatives. As she was with the rookie recruits and nursing staff, many of whom hoped that they would never have to enter this place ever again! She would gently tell them, eyebrows raised, they may just get the one more visit.......eventually!

She didn't tend to tell many what she did for a living. Mainly because people wanted to know what the work entailed, then when she began to tell them the truth, she could see them squirm, or light up with a strange morbid curiosity.

Her nickname was Morticia, she didn't mind. If she were feeling particularly impish and saw someone staring at her as she came out of the mortuary doors, she would pretend to shadow her eyes, squint at the light, put her dark glasses on and quickly run to her car! If they wanted to believe there was something vampire-like or ghoulish in there, that was their problem. The mortuary was named ward 13 (unlucky for some?) but not for her.

Katy had taken the job there because.... she had actually   feared   dying.

Bizarre as it sounded, it had helped her to come to terms with her own mortality... well, sort of. Some years ago a couple of friends she'd known had died young, far too soon, she couldn't get her head round it. She desperately wanted to understand that it was nothing personal.

To understand death, was to understand life and if you know you have no way of avoiding the first, then you must definitely get on and enjoy the latter!

She was in mid-twenties, single, loved her family, her independence and dancing. She was fit, healthy and enjoying life and hopefully, that's how it would stay, until some bloke she falls for gets in on the act and mucks it all up again.

She made a point of telling anyone, who asked her if she was scared of the bodies, ghosts, etc. 'You should always be far more scared of the living, than the dead.'

"Katy, is the DI in yet?" Beth whispered. Katy grinned, "You're okay I gave him a cup of tea, he and DS Lawson are in the backroom with Eric, checking details in the book." Beth gave her the knowing look. "And is DS Lawson still checking if you're single, you know he'll keep asking?" Katy smiled wryly.

Chappie spluttered. "Is that the DI you're on about? God, I hope not, we'd have to send a search party out if she got lost in that moustache!"

Katy turned and winced at Chappie then added shyly "DS Lawson is still asking me out at regular intervals, if I could get over past history, I'd probably shock him and me and accept."

"Go for it girl, there aren't many blokes who can say they're going out with a little beauty like you…......who removes people's internal organs for examination, then sews them back up with a hide needle and twine! Aslong as you don't go home in that get-up though, bit like dating the Slaughterers Apprentice!!"

Katy walks back into the PM room pulling on a new pair of gloves she looks at Chappie, her large eyes narrowing over the facemask. "Just remember what I do here, six or seven times in a morning, I'm a dab hand with a scalpel and rib-shears."

Beth chuckles as she sees Chappie wrinkle his nose, pulling a pained expression. The back room door opens, DI Hayman, DS Lawson and Mr Lewis, the forensic pathologist appear, Eric gives a thumbs up to Katy to prepare.

Mr Lewis waves his hand towards the SOCO officer, Pete Miller who is ready and waiting for the procedure to start.

"Pete have you taken your preliminary photos of the body, can we begin? Katy, is my board set up, are you going to be able assistant and help with this one?"

Cameron Lewis strides up to the body snapping his gloves into place and peering over his half-moon specs. A handsome, chiselled man for his age, with a positive main of grey hair.

"No problem Mr Lewis, everything's ready, sample jars, containers for hair samples, nail scrapings, swabs, all here. I've put your board up near the scales for organ weight, your ruler, inch markers and magnifier are all here on the slab side."

"Right, let's see if we can't find enough bits and bobs to point us in the right direction of the poor excuse for a human being that committed this appalling crime." Amen to that, Beth thinks, as she wills the pathologist to come up with some evidence.

"Elderly Caucasian, female, 4 feet 10 inches in height. There are some signs of rheumatoid arthritis in the fingers, on both hands, cataract in the right eye and some initial signs of malnutrition. Not that unusual, for someone of this age and living alone. Have we got the medication there?"

DS Lawson jumps as he's nudged by the DI, his attention focused on the petite, efficient, green and white flash that passes everything to the pathologist without being asked, that makes notes of figures, observations and......... has the most beautiful brown eyes...

"Sorry sir, I was err...just...err...here sir, the medication for Doris Linton."

Katy glances over quickly, he can tell by her eyes, even just over the top of her mask, she's smiling, probably thinks he's a right pillock.

"Auranofin, quite a few packs of aspirin and some....Isosorbide...er.... dinitrate sir?" Mr Lewis begins to study the bruising, putting small measure labels next the wounds, standing back to allow Pete to photograph each.

"So, going by her medication, when we finally get inside to the heart we may find, narrowing of the arteries pointing to angina, or signs of heart disease. We have her dentures there, apparently in a pot in the bathroom. It would seem she had removed them for soaking, before going to bed, which would tally with SOCO's findings so far, that the whole assault took place in the bedroom."

Chappie seemed agitated. "Don't you mean rape and murder sir? It was hardly just an assault." Chappie then found himself turning away. Even though it was a dead body before him, he couldn't help but feel ashamed and intrusive at having to witness the pathologist taking samples, scrapings and swabs from every orifice while they talked over the corpse.

"I'm sorry DC Chapman, but there appear to be no signs of asphyxia, no marks on the neck, or throat, no signs of fibres etc, in the nose or mouth, no blue-ness to the lips. I'm just checking the larynx here…Of course we will check the eyes and the brain but so far there appear to be no signs of baticial haemorrhaging either.

Cameron Lewis and Katy continue their efficient routine, searching, dissecting, carefully going over every inch of the body and its workings within. He finally puts down his instruments, sighs, while removing his gloves and apron. Katy reassembles the pale shell and its contents that once contained a life. Carefully finishing the stitching unobtrusively and washing down the body, gently washing Doris's hair, as if she were just asleep. It mattered to Katy…...that even in death, there should be dignity and consideration.

They left her to finish off. DS Lawson touched her shoulder as he passed. "Thank you, you make these ordeals so much easier for us." He accepts the gentle gaze from her warm brown eyes and sees his chance.

"Any chance 1 can take you mind off this job sometime? Maybe on the twentieth time of asking if I'm lucky?" He hears a faint chuckle from under her mask, as he winks and walks away.

As Cameron Lewis grabs his case to disappear in the office to complete paperwork, he turns to the officers awaiting his findings.

"Right then chaps, sadly, I think you've got your work cut out for you here. I can't give you the news you want to hear I'm afraid. Poor Doris Linton did have angina, but her arteries were further narrowed by atherosclerosis, signs of hypertension in the left ventricle, to put it simply, her heart would have been sufficiently impaired and with such severe shock and trauma, sadly led to a myocardial infarction which proved fatal."

DI Hayman puffed out his chest. "So, what you're saying Cameron is...he didn't actually kill her? Well, not intentionally?" Mr Lewis gazed over his notes.

"She was a frail 82year old, he attacked her, breaking her radius and her femur. She had severe internal bleeding around the pelvis, extensive external bruising, there are signs of attempted rape, though until lab results return, I can't say for certain if penetration took place. During this violent and degrading attack she died due to shock and severe trauma and the condition of her poor heart. To the vast majority we'd consider it murder, but to a defence lawyer it's an assault, possibly rape, but the suspect will say, that he did not intend to kill her."

"So, we have to try and gather enough evidence to try and prove otherwise?" Chappie grits his teeth and narrows his mouth. "Who's to say he wouldn't have finished her off if she hadn't died that way, who is to say he doesn't assume he killed her?"

The DI bristled. "Well, the only way we find that out, is by finding the suspect, quickly. Right, I want all officers at a briefing at 6pm. Can we get some of those early actions out of the way. Let's give some statements the once over. What about this dustbin man who found the body, we need to get more details on his background......"

"Okay sir, we'll get off, I'll contact the incident room see what we've got so far." Beth and Chappie breathed in deeply as they stepped outside.

"The bastard who did this is just laughing at us, knowing full well we can't pin murder on him. Rape, assault, six years maybe, four, for good behaviour?"

"Good behaviour! What sort of claptrap is that! How many old ladies will he have in prison to have a go at? Just because he creeps around prison, tugging his forelock at the officers, doesn't mean there isn't a cruel, perverted, deceitful little raddled brain still lurking in that malformed head of his. Just waiting to be released, to commit the same bloody crimes all over again."

Beth pats Chappie's arm gently, then tugs his sleeve. "Come on, remember, we're not allowed to have opinions we just do the laws dirty work, we get it right sometimes and we get it chucked back in our faces on others. We just have to try and do our best for the victims and their families. Come on, we'll nip to the Incident Room and see if any names are being bandied about, see what we've got to go on."

Chapter 7

Ken tentatively tapped on the door, lifting the letterbox he peered into the hallway. "Harry! I've got yer bike here mate, I brought it back from the depot, are you okay?" He turns the handle slowly, the door opens.

"Harry, I just wanted to say...well, me and the boys.......just....you know......we're so sorry you had to see...." Ken turned into the small front room, the big friendly giant of a man was sitting, rocking back and forth, his arms locked around his knees, gazing at a picture of his mum. His eyes were red and blood-shot. Ken swallowed hard as he took in the pathetic sight.

He looked up at Ken, his lip trembling. "You know they get old, unwell, frail, but no one....no one...should have to end their life like that. I can't believe another human being could be so vile, to such a gentle soul. She'd have been no threat.... he didn't have to…...I just can't believe...." Harry's shoulders hunched as the tears flowed again, he quickly turned his head so Ken wouldn't see him sobbing.

"Look big man, I'll put the kettle on, make us a nice strong brew. Hey, your mum or Mrs Linton, wouldn't want you to forget Billy here, he's pushing his empty bowl round the kitchen." Ken stroked the head of the hungry, confused cat.

Ken jumped, as there was a loud knock at the door. "I'll get it Harry, don't worry." As he opened the door two plain clothed officers were holding up their ID cards. "Detective Sergeant Radford and this is Detective Constable Davies are you Harold Robinson?" Ken backed away gesturing a hand towards the front room.

"No, I'm his boss, Ken Briggs ...err...what... he's in there."

The two officers walked straight into the front room and stood in front of Harry as his red-rimmed eyes stared up at them. "Harold Robinson, we would like you to come with us to the station for questioning over the death of Doris Linton, you are not under arrest, but we would like all items of clothing you were wearing this morning when you found the body."

Harry swallowed hard, then stood up slowly. Ken stepped forward.

"He found the body for God's sake. He's not long been back from giving his witness statement. Malcolm said he was barely in that house five minutes. You don't believe for one minute he had anything to do with this?"

"I'm sorry Mr Briggs, we're just doing our job, Mr Robinson is only being taken for questioning, his

113

evidence could be vital to this inquiry." They bagged up his overalls and work boots, then his work coat, as Harry pointed to it on the peg.

"I wore that, it was chilly this morning...."

As Harry climbed into the police car a wave of nausea hit him, as he recalls Ken's words. Suddenly he realised they obviously thought him a possible suspect, that *he* might have committed this appalling crime.

As he passed the Resource Centre on his way back to the interview room, DC Davies popped his head in. "Helen love, can you try and get a message to Nigel, suspect's just hoyed up in the back of the new Peugeot, I'll leave the keys on the board. Get him to clean it ASAP, we'll need it within the hour, leave it with you gorgeous and if you see DS Radford tell him we're in interview room 3. Thanks sweetheart."

Helen smiled politely as she tried Nigel's number....

She was trying to decide which made *her* feel more nauseous, condescending over friendly officers, or cleaning someone else's sick from the back of a car? Hard choice she thought, smiling to herself.

As DS Radford eventually appeared, the officers were almost overpowered by his sudden watt of aftershave. DC Davies tucking his hand swiftly but casually under his nose, to soften the smell and stop himself from sniggering as he catches sight of his DS's expression at the possibility of vomit residue on Harry.

Harry listened as DS Radford asked him things about his family, his past, then they asked him about his mother. Why had he moved back? How close had he been to his mother? Did he possibly have a mother fixation? Did he miss his mother? Had he seen Doris Linton as a surrogate mother? And how close had he been to Doris Linton?

He sat patiently, trying to answer their questions honestly, without getting angry, but he was finding it more and more distasteful as to what they seemed to be implying.

"I can't believe what you're trying to suggest here. *I* found her body. *I* rang the police. Her poor cat, she loved those cats, lying there, bones broken and her...... the same way. How...how on earth can you think I could do something so vile?" Harry put his head in his hands and broke down.

"I'm sorry Mr Robinson, but we have to establish the facts."

Harry looked up, tears streaming, upset, angry and feeling very vulnerable. "Well, establish these facts. I lost my dad at 16yrs old, who I loved dearly, I also love my sister and my mum, 'till the day she died. I'm 48yrs old, I have a job, I pay my way. I have friends and a social life. I've never had a girlfriend who was more than two years older than me. I can give you all their names just in case you want to check my sexual habits. I ride a bicycle, listen to Terry Wogan and enjoy a good comedy on TV. I don't trawl the internet, I don't stalk old ladies and I don't read the Sun newspaper, I prefer The Mail ...if this paints me as a sadistic, perverted, rapist and killer of the elderly, then God help 60% of the nation!"

DS Radford leaned forward. "Who said Doris Linton had been raped, Harry?" Harry closed his eyes tight, to try and stop the tears. "Because she, because I...I..."

"What did you do Harry...eh? What did you do?" DS Radford smirked sideways giving a look to DC Davies as if to say, this is it, they all break eventually.

Harry took a deep breath. "When I went into the room she was lying there, on the bed, she was covered in awful bruises. Horrible bruises, all over her poor, broken body, including her legs, above her knees….on her thigh. I thought he must have........I could see because...because her night-dress had been pulled right up…. up under her chin."

Harry bit his lip, remembering the traumatic sight. "I pulled her night-gown down...... just to cover her up......I know I shouldn't have touched anything, but I couldn't leave her like that ... I couldn't...... it was so undignified, disrespectful so...so disrespectful."

"You didn't touch anything else then Harry?" Harry tried to stay calm.

"No, I didn't, well only the phone, but that was to ring you lot, I touched nothing else." DS Radford leaned forward again. "What about the outside light you went to change?"

118

Harry looked straight at him. "As I told the policeman this morning, the light worked, someone else must have changed it! It didn't work last week, she showed me. She said if she got the bulb, would I put it for her. Why would I lie? I was there to change the bulb and collect the rubbish, that's all."

Harry looked at the officer in despair. "I can't believe you're still in here. Why aren't you out there, getting the bastard who did this? I'm telling you, if I find him first, I'll kill the cowardly shit, I will...I'll kill him...." Harry broke down, his head in his hands falling forward onto the table, sobbing.

Kenny Radford, emotionless, stood up and walked towards the door.

"Right then Mr Robinson you're free to go for now, don't leave the country. You don't live far away you can find your own way home I assume? Walk will do you good...eh? Good man. PC

119

Dean, will you kindly show this ...gentleman out when he's ready, *we* must get to the briefing at HQ."

Chapter 8

"Mim...Mim! The little shit! He's ad me last tenner out the pot! Mim...Mim!"

Earl is going red in the face with anger. Unable to get himself up easily, he flails in the chair, like some large, like a large, upturned tortoise.

"Fer Christ's sake keep yer fuckin 'air on yer big gob-shite. D'ya want the whole estate t'know you think yer own son's a thief!" Mim lights two cigarettes, passing one to Earl, who looks as if he's about to have a seizure.

"I don't mean our Liam! I mean that thieving twat Dabber. Our Duke was the same when we were lads, always nickin' me stuff, anything he could sell, gone.

Look at his bloody kids, all the same, but Dwayne's the worst, evil little...." Mim chucked the paper at him to shut him up.

"Your whole family are the same, not just Duke and his boys. Three bloody times you were in! Or'ave yer bloody magnesia, or summat...eh?" She pulls two stained mugs from the sink and clicks the kettle on.

"We did burglaries to help us live, get a meal on the table, these shits nowadays it's all SLD, sniffing this, taking that, bloody needles an all, it's not fuckin right Mim, it's not fuckin' right...."

Mim turned, staring at the man she'd loved and given her all to at 17yrs old, the handsome, cheeky, wide-boy she'd fallen for and stayed with, no matter what.

"Earl, wasting 'arf yer life in prison is not fuckin' right! No matter what you've done and 'owever yuv dunnit....it wer still against the law! Ere av a cup a tea darl read yer paper. The lads will 'av just stayed at Stacey's...and before yer blow another bloody ar'try, she's gone on them contraceptic injections in 'er bum to stop 'er 'aving anymore kids."

"Well, that's one bloody needle that's doing some good then, feel sorry for the poor fucker that's got to go near that heifers backside!" He grunts, disappearing into his newspaper.

Mim clatters up the un-carpeted stairs, peering round the door of Liam's room hoping he may have sneaked back in while they were talking. He's a good lad, Liam. Just soft sometimes, lets that Dwayne and Stacey take a lend, it's not right. She sees his holdall is gone and his best jeans off the back of the chair. Hope he's gone for that job, not off with Dwayne...sure way to mess everything up, taking that trout-head with him. She straightens the bedding, flicking the ash and as it drops onto the floor, she treads it into the carpet. She hopes that

Liam is one member of the Dalby family that may, just may, stay out of trouble.

In Central Avenue the door is open for business, although there is only Shell who's conscious. A thick pink, towelling bathrobe, tied tightly under her bust, making sure as she passes the spare room she leans in, her breasts swinging freely underneath. As Dabber pulls himself half up to grab the mug of tea from her, he sees a flash of nipple, giving him an instant hard on.

"Fancy a quickie Shell? Come on babe..." He says, grabbing at her thigh. She looks at the skinny specimen, not exactly David Beckham, or 50 Cents when she's sober, but at least he's eager and can stay awake for the five minutes it usually takes. Better than now't she thinks, as she unties her robe and slides under the duvet.

Minutes later. "Fuckin' 'ell babe you don't arf go at it, I can't stop mesel' when yer on top" She climbs off, smiling to herself, never to waste an opportunity, to get what she wanted. She ties herself in again then disappears to the bathroom.

He can hear the shower running, a thought passes briefly through his head, but he reaches over and lights up a ciggie instead. Can't give 'er too much of a good thing he thinks, smirking to himself.

He leans back into the pillow, the previous night seeming a distant memory, all the same he thinks, maybe better lie low for a couple of days. He had money to spend, there were plenty of tabs, fixes of every kind here, no probs. No way was he going back to Liam's, Earl would have him grassed up and out sharpish, the fat bastard.

DI Hayman clears his throat and runs a single finger under his thick moustache, standing in front of the evidence boards. Chappie leans towards several colleagues, who are still perusing witness statements. "Bit of hush lads, old Wahay has just landed, his flaps are down, so listen up."

"Right, are we all here? I have a feeling this not going to be as straightforward as we'd hoped, so we really have to pull together, pool resources and information. We need to communicate, liaise and discuss! Is that clear?" Several had trouble not saluting and shouting, 'Sir, yes sir!'

"We have here, an *abhorrent* attack on a frail elderly lady, which very traumatically ended in her death. We do not want the person who did this to evade justice, but whatever our own feelings are on this......apparently......as a result of the post-mortem, it is not murder, but we would like to get manslaughter at the very least." There is a ripple of noise and under the breath remarks. He continues.

"We do need as much evidence as possible to prove this suspect's obvious intentions, so that when he is caught, we can get him put away for as long as possible. Do we all understand that?" He never doubted what his officers were thinking and feeling, whatever the court delivered, would be nowhere near what this piece of scum deserved.

"We have fingerprint results, hopefully coming through tomorrow morning. Although SOCO have told us they found glove marks, inverted, on the rear transom window, we do have prints from elsewhere in the house, and on the outside lightbulb. Maybe he was a bogus official, made a previous call to give the place the once over, an odd job man. We have to hope we have his fingerprints somewhere. We have other items for possible DNA. I believe he may have drunk from a milk carton which was found empty, is that right Pete?" He peers over his specs towards the SOCO officer.

"Yes sir. It'll be sometime next week before the lab have anything on that though. But we've taken cat fur samples, fibres etc, so if we get any suspects in, in the meantime we've got possible transference to go on."

Chappie pipes up, "Nice one Pete, trans... 'fur'....ance....cats...get it?"

As several started to laugh, the DI coughed loudly. "Yes, yes, I realise we need to relieve the stress but a time and a place people...time and a place."

He turns to look at the photographs on the board, taken by SOCO of the crime scene. "We have to focus, we have to try and work out what we have here, what sort of person could do this." He points at the photo of a frail body, prostrate across her floral bedding.

Beth again, bites her lip, she thinks of the family, of all the families, who have never known what further appalling humiliation their loved ones suffer, even after death. Kate had rung minutes before, from the mortuary, to say Mr Beech had come up with a police officer to identify Doris Linton. She said he'd been so grateful as she looked so...at peace. Here we were, days, maybe weeks or months, many officers and forensic experts coming in and out to look at the poor soul in these pictures, looking anything, but at peace.

"I have consulted with some of you and with Aykley Heads, also Wetherby labs. We all have lots of work to do, lots of actions to pursue. Any likely suspects must be dealt with quickly if we have any chance of forensics, so please get those lists checked. We've got Caroline Palmer, our analyst for this run, checking MO and areas etc. We need names checking on CRO. Has anyone got anything worth discussing as yet?"

Kenny Radford tapped his pen on his clipboard loudly. "Sir, we've actually had the….'Waste Disposal Operative' in again, for questioning." The DI looks puzzled, "Sorry, who was that?"

"Err...Harry Robinson, he found the body sir." The DI stepped forward. "Waste Disposal Operative? He's a bloody dustman, a bin-man, dear God Radford, we'll have none of this namby-pamby PC clap trap in here. How many women do that job...eh? It's a dustman, or bin-man, till I see otherwise, then it'll be a dust-woman or bin-woman! Bloody 'Waste Disposal Operative....jeez" He exasperates, looking skywards.

DS Radford flushes scarlet but carries on. "Well, we see him as a prime suspect sir. We feel he should be kept under obs sir. He certainly knew the deceased, had the opportunity and the motive. He's late forties, living alone, no female company."

The DI raised his eyebrows. "Well Radford, think you need a bit more than that to charge him, otherwise Middlesbrough cells are going to get a bit crowded over the next couple of days, possibly including a couple of our own officers." There were a couple of sniggers from the back of the room. Kenny shuffled awkwardly in his seat.

"Yes, I realise that sir, we have several avenues to explore." The DI smiled. "A to Z handy then Radford? Don't want you losing your way on this one. That goes for all of you. This is one of those despicable crimes and everyone wants to get whoever did it as soon as possible. But remember, tread softly and carefully, we need names, we need information but most importantly for the CPS and courts to take it up, we need evidence. Next briefing at 9pm. As I always say, you don't need good luck, you need good policing... thank you everyone."

Beth strode quickly over to Kenny. "I can't believe you think it's Harry Robinson. He was distraught this morning." Kenny swaggered slightly.

"Oh, come on Beth, we've seen it all before, Gordon Wardell, there amongst it all, feigning shock and grief, it's part of the act the buzz of seeing how many people they can dupe. Look at Jeremy Bamber, even put the blame on one of his victims. We get Robinson in again in a couple of days and he'll be saying the old bird threw herself at him and tried to seduce him... stranger things have happened."

Beth turned away in disgust. "Have some respect Kenny and just stick to the facts. He was at work, his work colleagues were yards away, he didn't have time to do what was done in there. Read the notes from his boss, he was heartbroken when his dad died, let alone nursing his mother till she died of cancer. He had nothing but admiration and kindness   towards the elderly."

132

Beth didn't even want to hear his answer she hurried away towards the stairs. She caught up with Chappie and Pud.

"Come on you two, it's obviously going to be up to us to prove the 'Blues Brothers' wrong. I'm going to see Jim in LIO see who we've got on file, similar MO, etc. Chappie, will you and Pud just go to Tyrone Stock's address. Apparently, one of the actions states he's always hanging about the Post Office. He may know something. But judging by all the young girls he hangs about with, I can't see him being involved. OAP's aren't really his thing, but he may have heard a whisper. You know how the jungle drums beat around here, even the criminal fraternity find this sort of crime a touch sick."

"Beth, what can I do for you my lovely." Jim smiled warmly flicking through files between sups from a very, large mug of strong tea. He was part of the furniture, always well-polished, but showing a little sign of wear around the edges. He was the walking oracle of local intelligence. His brain was an amazing memory bank of names, faces, addresses, associates, going back donkeys' years. He rarely used the computer. They insisted he had to update his system, he didn't need to. He *was* the system.

"Jim, I've got an action to follow up, anonymous caller has given two local burglars names, they use the same MO as last nights break. They both have some previous for violence in the area, just wondered if you have any current addresses I can check?" Beth passes a piece of paper to Jim.

"Do you want me to do the full bifter on the compy? Only, you'll have to give me some time, I can't get the hang of the new thingy they've put on. Supposed to make things easier, huh! If him up there had wanted us to use computers, he'd have given us two fingers on each hand and a head the size of a golf-ball, what d'you reckon?"

Beth chuckled, "Haven't you just described someone we know? Honestly Jim, I trust your local knowledge totally, just give me the current, from the top of your.........baseball sized head!"

Jim roared with laughter, took a slurp from his tea and deftly flicked through his files. "Right, who've you got here, Gary, 'Gazza' Madden, IC 1, 5ft 9", light brown hair, currently with blonde streaks, never out of his white tracksuit. Two kids to Thelma Banks but after domestic violence on which she finally pressed charges after he broke her jaw, he is now living with her 19year old cousin, Chasnay-Rae Jackson who he has just generously fertilised. Now giving her the prospect of one in every colour!"

"My God Jim, it's better than any soap opera coming in here! How the vast majority of our world live eh! Nothing, if not varied, yuck...and the address of this violent criminal, father to be, contributor to the next generation?" Beth gritted her teeth at the appalling prospect.

"Jim pulled out a card quickly turning it towards her. "Number 10a Franks Court, St. Hildas, its Social Housing. Naturally, he hasn't got time to work. He signs on Tuesday after 1pm, if he's not at home address. He was last in for a break two weeks ago. He's fairly prolific what with a drug and drink habit, a new girlfriend to impress and another kid on the way. Naturally, they can feed it on free powdered milk and greasy sausage rolls, but of course you have to be pushing the poor, premature, asthmatic thing round in the same buggy as the Beckhams, when you're showing off its designer baby-grow and solid gold creole earrings. So of course you need a bit of added cash to bulk out your benefits."

Jim looked at her sideways. "Oh dear, am I being a tad cynical here?"

"Sadly not." Beth said, sighing deeply. Was it just the biased and blinkered world she worked in? Or was the country really, as bad as it appeared? This job certainly worked as a good contraceptive to her. Apart from never having the time, or inclination to procreate for pleasure, the thought of bringing a life into this over-crowded, unfriendly, uncaring, selfish country, of dishonest vile people, was not a prospect she cherished. Would she ever feel she had done enough to regain her faith in society? Well, this time she would certainly try her hardest.

Jim smiled across at her, he'd poured her a cup of tea and pushed a packet of her favourite Jaffa Cakes toward her. He then spoke gently, sensing her weariness.

"Eh lass, take the weight off your sling-backs for ten minutes my lovely, while I get the rest of the info for you."

"You are a saint Jim, here's the other....'Gentleman of this parish.' Got anything recent on him?" Beth pointed to the other name. Jim's face grimaced.

"Nasty piece of work that one, came to light about six months ago, Dwayne Prince Dalby. Nickname, 'Dabber'. The family's Royal connections are in name only, which will be a relief to her majesty, except for languishing in her prisons on regular intervals."

Jim chuckles again, then straightens up quickly. "Street robberies, most with violence and a prolific burglar with a 'goes without saying', drug habit to feed. 5ft 3, skinny ratty looking thing, tattoo of a spider on his left forearm. Windows his usual POE and MO, but usually wears gloves, so difficult to pin down. He's managed to get off with most of them, due to lack of evidence. Let's see what me card says."

Flipping out the beige cards, he shuffles them like a dealer at a casino.

"Ah, he's due at Teesside Magistrates on the 20th of this month, might be worth a visit if you can't find him at an address. He's NFA according to this, but he gave his Uncle Earl's as a bail address, 104 Granville Road, Grangetown."

Beth glances at the calendar, 20th, that's this coming Monday,

"That's a bit of luck if we can't get hold of him before, maybe we'll have some forensics back by then too. Thanks Jim, I owe you one." He points at the second Jaffa Cake just reaching her mouth. "Two actually, we'll say one free with each suspect, that okay my lovely."

"Beth....If you have no luck, just come see me and my baseball sized head again. Dalby's associates......who help him sell his stolen gear......hang on...hang on....it's coming to me...Kieron Parker, 'Kizzer', his wife's name is......Shelly. Just had her in last week, shoplifting again. Central Avenue....number 29...not that far from your crime scene actually."

Beth made notes quickly and stuffs the paper into her pocket.

"Thanks, I'll tread carefully, you know what they're like, go in too heavy handed and their defence will rip us apart. I'll try and get some forensic through first, I want this...specimen......piece of......suspect, well and truly nailed, through the head would be nice, but not an option, sadly."

Chapter 9

"DC Chapman, come in please......Can I have your ETA back to the office." Beth speaks quickly, but clearly, clutching the police radio impatiently.

"ETA to M1 fifteen minutes, just finishing a statement." Beth smiles to herself. "Thank you, DC Chapman, see you in twenty." She glances at the clock. It's after 6.30pm, they'll be getting some food on the way back, Chappie won't last till the briefing at 9pm, without copious amounts of monosodium glutamate.

She was still smiling when her desk phone rang. "Hello, DS Flynn, Middlesbrough CID, can I help you?" It was a few seconds before someone spoke. "Er, they put me through to you, are you on the murder case?" Beth reached for a pad, and paper. "Yes, but switchboard should have put you through to the incident room, can I take your name?"

Beth's heart sank as he spoke. "It's....it's Harry Robinson, er, I found Mrs Linton's body...er...you had me in for questioning...." Beth quickly interrupted.

"Mr Robinson don't say any more, if you want to add anything to your statement, consider carefully if you need a solicitor......"

She heard quiet sniffles and a tremble in his voice.

"Not you as well...... I didn't hurt her, I would never have hurt her......I was just wanting to ask if I could have my work coat back......I need it..... my gate keys are in the pockets.......I have to unlock the alley gates to get the bins out. I just need my keys......for work on Monday."

Beth bit her lip, God she was becoming so cynical, she knew this man wasn't capable of such a foul crime and yet she almost believed he was ringing to confess.

"I'm so sorry Mr Robinson, I've been dealing with so many......statements today. I didn't realise DS Radford had taken your coat, I'll let him know of the keys in the pocket and we'll get them back to you before Monday."

"Thank you very much. I should be in most of the weekend, I've got me chores to do, but I go up the cemetery around 2pm on Sunday, to visit mum and dad's grave, tidy up, leave flowers, will that be okay?"

"Of course, Mr Robinson. I understand, I try and visit my Grans as often as I can, unless my shifts dictate otherwise. It's a way of staying close to them isn't it. Grandpa was killed in the war so I never knew him, but I was so close to my gran......" Beth realises she's not being very professional, letting her emotions take over.

"Right, okay then Mr Robinson, we should be able to get your keys back to you tomorrow. Bye for now." She pressed the receiver to her head, banging it a couple of times as if chastising herself for her show of weakness.

"Might have known you'd be in here. Have you not left your desk in the last two hours? All work and no play, makes Beth a very dull girl."

Beth raised her eyebrows at Chappie.

"Well, you'd know wouldn't you. All play and no work, makes Chappie a very skint and knackered boy!" Chappie passes her a sandwich, as the boys unwrap their chips.

"If only! I'd happily be skint and knackered if someone would just make it worth me while…….." He winks suggestively at Beth.

"Don't look at me sweetheart, I'm far too dull to even have a clue what you're talking about. Now eat your chips and tell me if your chat with Tyrone Stocks was worth the effort."

Chappie and Pud pull up their chairs, pocket-books in one hand, chips in the other. "Well, Sarge, as far as we can ascertain, Stocks had seen Doris Linton on Tuesday calling at the post office. I mean he knows of her by sight, but he just refers to her as, 'one of the oldies getting their pension.' He also mentioned he helps his great gran with her shopping. He doesn't seem in that league, he doesn't seem the violent type at all. Uniform said they've only had him in for a caution, underage drinking and graffiti."

Pud then flicks open his pocket-book. "The other factor is he doesn't appear to have many male friends, but the local girls love him. Don't think it's in the romantic way either, I think it's for his advice on fashion and hair colour."

Beth chirps in quickly. "Remember Norman Bates in Psycho, controlling female influenced his outlook on life, does great gran force him to help with the shopping, or is it voluntary?"

Chappie pulls a face. "Norman Bates was fictitious, he seems to love his great gran and her cats, she's got four. He helps carry all the cat food home, mad about them, he named them all." Beth feigns puzzlement. "Who, Norman Bates?"

Chappie sighs, shutting his pocket-book. "DC Ambrose, I feel our information should be given to the Incident Room, where professional police persons are awaiting our actions and our efficient work ethics...."

Beth sniggers as Pud tries to stuff his last six chips in while trying to verbalise his agreement. Chappie

146

slaps his forehead in exasperation. "You can't get the bloody staff, can you? What the hell have I got as a sidekick, a Gloucester Old Spot in a suit!"

Beth can't help but laugh loudly. "Right, sit down now, both of you and I'll tell you what I got. Contrary to popular belief, I did leave this office. Been down to see Jim in LIO and got a couple of addresses worth checking. I've also been passed an action to speak to a Mr Charlton, lives opposite Mrs Linton, saw a male in a long dark coat, just as it was getting light on Wednesday morning. He says it looked like he was doing something with the light at the side of the house. So, I say we pop round for a quick chat now, before the briefing and get a full description. It might help evidence wise if we do get a name to the fingerprints on the bulb."

"Who is it please." A frail voice called out from the other side of the door.

147

"DS Flynn, DC Chapman and DC Ambrose, is that Mr Charlton? You spoke to the Incident Room this afternoon about a man at Mrs Linton's house early Wednesday morning."

The letterbox opened. "Can you show some form of identification please." Beth begins to root through her handbag for her ID card, not often asked for, strangely enough she thinks.

Pud looks worried. "I've left mine at the office." He whispers.

Beth pushes her card through the letterbox. A few seconds later, it's pushed back through. DC Chapman does the same. "Didn't you say there were three of you." Chappie looks skyward then posts his ID card back through.

"Worth a try, otherwise we'll have to come back with the Gloucester Old Spots tomorrow." But the card comes back through and the door opens.

"I didn't get a very good look at him, I didn't really see his face, my Lilac blocked the view." Pud looks confused. "That your wife sir?" He smiles sympathetically. "No, Detective Constable, it's the tree in the front garden."

"If you could give us an approximate height, description of clothing sir. You told the officer in the Incident Room, that he wore a long coat?"

Mr Charlton sat down slowly, thinking carefully. "He was quite tall, a good six foot I'd say. Dark hair…...he was wearing one of those smart raincoats, like city gents wear, a dark colour, navy or black. Just seemed odd at that time in the morning, must have been about half five. I was just opening my curtains. I'm always up at five, I like to listen to our dawn chorus see."

Before Pud could speak, Chappie whispered. "No Pud, she's not a DJ on Radio 2, Dawn Chorus, is birdsong...." Pud gives a sideways glare. "Ay, I know, I know."

"You have been a great help Mr Charlton, thank you very much."

Beth gets up from the threadbare sofa. Mr Charlton touched her arm gently. "I wished I'd helped a bit more, since Arthur went. But I didn't want her to feel awkward, I didn't want neighbours gossiping. You know, us both being widowed. She was a proper lady was Mrs Linton....Dotty......dreadful what happened to her ....dreadful. Would you let me know...you know when her funeral is.......I'd like to pay my respects." Beth touched the old man's shoulder in return. "Thank you again Mr Charlton, we'll let you know."

Chappie drove while Beth finished her notes for the briefing. "I can't really see a six-foot man in a long dark coat, dressed like a city gent, squeezing himself through that transom window can you?" Both lads shaking their heads were thinking carefully over the details.

"Maybe there were two of them, to set it all up." Pud said with little conviction to his thought. "Why would two go to all that trouble though, there was little security, no reason for them to suspect there was any great wealth there, to make it worthwhile planning it all to the enth degree.......I just can't see it."

"We have to stay focused. We'll get this briefing out the way, see if anyone else has got any more to go on, then we'll get home, get an early night, we need our wits about us tomorrow. Fresh day, fresh minds eh boys? So, Chappie, make sure you spray yours with something to neutralise *your* fresh thoughts."

"Oh, ha, ha...there's nothing wrong with my mind, just needs a soft cloth and a bit of Dettol, mmmm...Dettol...medical......nurses.....See, total logic there!"

They couldn't help but laugh, they had to do whatever kept them going, whatever kept them alert on their twelve hour plus shifts for the next few weeks.

If they were laughing, they were still awake.

Forty minutes later they left the Incident Room tired and slightly deflated. "Well, there wasn't much to go on from that briefing. I think we're all just scratching the surface at the moment. Got a couple of addresses to visit tomorrow, so we'll see if they can shed any light. See you early doors boys."

Back at the station Beth went through to the custody office.

The desk Sgt was busy booking in a rowdy male, who was banging his fist on the counter and swearing loudly as two PC's tried to gently help him remove anything of harm. The prisoner was obviously high, drunk, or both and tried to kick one of the officers, then made the mistake of trying to get the female officer into a headlock. Within seconds he was flat on the floor, eyes wide with shock and winded. Handcuffed and subdued he went quietly to a cell. As his cell door was closed, the female officer spoke calmly with a gentle Scottish lilt.

"Have yersel' forty winks luvvy, I'll get you a cup of tea okay."

"Streuth Maggie, I thought it was supposed to be one or the other, good cop *or* bad cop, not both rolled into one!" Beth grinned at PC Creel.

"Oh away we yer, he's a big softie, poor sod. It's all in the drink. He lost his wifey in that house fire on George Street last year, *his* cigarette caused it, never bin the same. Ye canna blame the poor bugger fer droonin' himsel in drink. I Think I'd do the same....but I'd make it a good Scotch malt, not that cheap cacky belly burnin' stuff he's bin on! His breath would strip paint!"

Beth admired the officer's strength of character. She remembers her own, when in uniform, all those years ago. She'd wanted to change the world, make a real difference, but as the injustice of it all became so apparent, she just wanted to prove there *was* a difference. That no matter what the media said about the force, the back biting, the hypocrisy, the lack of Government support, the lack of public trust, she did want to be a part of it, she did want to be here.........well most of the time.

Her thoughts were interrupted. "Well DS Flynn, stand there any longer and I'll have you done for loitering." Sergeant Baker peered over his glasses and smiled.

Sorry Bob, miles away and I should be...my bed is calling. I just wanted to know if DS Radford got in touch with you about the coat belonging to Harry Robinson. He'd had him in for questioning but didn't give him his work keys back. Has he sealed and labelled the bag for forensics? It's just Mr Robinson needs those keys, they're in a pocket apparently."

The Sgt got the keys for the evidence cupboard.

"Must be honest, Beth, Radford will do the bare minimum if he can get away with it. Only does forensics if he must, too much paperwork for him. I'm sure the bag wasn't sealed." He unlocked the cupboard and pulled out a large brown unsealed evidence bag." Beth sighed. She quickly grabbed a pair of latex gloves.

"Well, he's done a label, that's something. He's only written the coat on it, so he hasn't even checked the pockets. I'll take the keys, they're of no value except to Mr Harrison for work. I'll seal it up, while I've got my gloves on. I think Radford missed the evidence packaging course."

"You're too good to him Beth, he's slap dash, he could do with the warning, might shake him up a bit, bet he wouldn't cover your back as quick." He passed her a large roll of brown tape from the equipment case.

"Don't be too hard on him, he's been here a lot of years, then I just appear and arrest his two top targets within my first couple of months. He's just so desperate to re-instate his street cred, it's a man thing."

"Yeah, only to a macho fat-head like him! He should be grateful he's got the extra help up there. I sometimes think that office is full of dead-wood and young numptys." He shakes his head.

Beth looks at him with a sideways glance. "And which am I? A young numpty I hope? Didn't I hear you put in for CID a few years ago Bob?"

He laughed nudging her. "By heck, you and your woman's intuition. Yes okay, I'm bloody jealous! Especially when Radford the Prat is lording himself around, making his crass superior remarks about the difference between, 'the wooden-tops' and them upstairs. One more comment and I won't be responsible for where I stick his bottle of Jean Paul Gaultier!"

"Ooooh, sounds painful, especially with those funny shaped bottles! I'm going before you start resenting my presence too."

She puts on a superior upper-class voice. "Well Hudson, I'll just leave you, Mrs Bridges and Ruby to clean up down here and I'll be off upstairs to blow my nose on a lace handkerchief and be away to my four-poster, I bid you goodnight."

She heard Bob chuckling, she smiled, walking tiredly towards the door.

It was nearly eleven when she pulled into her drive. Freddie patiently waiting on the windowsill, legs crossed. He bounced in excitement as she reached for his lead. "Come on little buddy, let's have our walk, clear the mind, refresh the senses." She was trying to convince herself, but really, she was just too knackered to care.

Chapter 10

"It's Saturday mornin' for fuck's sake, can't even read me daily in peace! Don't fuckin' believe it, police are outside Mim....Mim! I told you that little shit would bring us nout but trouble." Earl was standing at the window, waving his paper, puffing on a cigarette as if it were his last. The sight of police officers had never brought out the best in him. He could hear Mim clattering down the stairs.

"You don't bloody know what they 'ere for, maybe summut's 'appened to our Liam, just shut it will you. Just bloody well shut it! Don't you 'av a go and get yer stroppy 'ed on Earl, or I'm off, d'you hear me!"

Mim opened the door on the second knock. "Christ, plain clothes and uniform bobbies, this isn't bad news is it?" Mim held herself in check.

Beth showed her ID. "Miriam Dalby, wife of Earl Dalby. Dwayne Dalby has your address as his last known. Is he living here at the moment?"

Earl had overheard and shouted through. "I knew that little shit would bring us trouble, bloody knew it!" Mim quickly ushered the officers in, seeing the neighbour's doors opening and kids hovering close by. The uniform officers stayed by the vehicles, knowing only too well, that depending on who was in the house and the outcome, they would get jeered, verbal abuse, but possibly more.

"We just need to speak to Dwayne, Mr Dalby. Just need to know his whereabouts for Thursday night into Friday morning." Earl grunted.

"Oh yeah, you just need to speak to him, because he may be a witness when a crime took place, he might have been talking quietly with friends, having a McDonalds with a some half decent girly from Acklam way. You must think we're fuckin' stupid! You obviously know the runt is up to his shifty little eyes in it."

"Earl, will you shut up, for crying out loud, what if something 'as happened to our Liam and he knows something, knows where he is, just shut up and listen!"

Mim offered the officers a seat, pushing off a sleepy Staffy and a pile of catalogues. Beth looked straight at Mrs Dalby. "Are you saying your son Liam is missing?"

"No, not missing......he's probably staying round at Stacey's, his kiddie's there, he'll 'av gone round hers more than likely. Can't see Dabber dossing there though, don't think she'd av 'im at her place."

"Dwayne and Stacey don't get on then, is that what you're saying?"

DC Chapman was taking notes. "She thinks he's a perv, always trying to get off with her mates. She's only a teen herself,' she 'as a lot of young 'uns round."

"So, he prefers the younger girls, does he?" Earl lets out another snort.

"You should 'ear 'im talk, you'd think he ad 'em falling all over 'im. He'd shag anything! Man, woman, or beast! Only one problem, they wouldn't 'ave 'im fuckin' gift-wrapped. He's a drugged up little tosser. He'll be holed up in some druggie mate's squat down Union Street. Go and knock on a few doors down there instead of hassling us, eh?"

"Earl shut up will you!" Mim swatted him with the newspaper.

"I want to know our Liam's safe." She turned and picked up a large pink leather bag.

"Stacey's got a flat in Ormesby. Hang on I'll get the address, go round there first. If our Liam's there, he'll know where Dwayne is. They went down the town together Thursday night. The lads said they were going to meet the lasses......me'be they didn't.....might 'av gone round a mates house.......what der yer reckon?"

Beth could sense that Mrs Dalby needed some reassurance.

"I think we should visit Stacey next. If Liam's is there, then he may have some info on Dwayne. Would you like us to ask Liam to get in touch Mrs Dalby?"

"Oh, I know yer busy like, he'll probably be home soon. We av a takeaway on a Saturday night, he'll

163

be back for that......well me'be tell 'im.....no, it's okay....thanks." Mim almost smiled at Beth, but caught Earl's eyes glaring at her, she got up to show them to the door.

DC Chapman drove across to North Ormesby. "Doesn't sound as if Dwayne Dalby's our man does it, if he's perving round this Stacey's young friends, what d'ya reckon."

DC Ambrose piped up "Yeah, but his uncle did say he didn't seem to get lucky, maybe he just decided to take it from someone who wouldn't, or couldn't, put up a fight." The two men visibly cringed. Beth stared out of the window, gritting her teeth.

"All the more reason to make sure, if it is him......that he's dealt with properly and quickly, don't you think?"

Beth climbed from the car, looking at the piece of paper with Stacey's address scribbled down by Mrs Dalby. "I think it says 13 Burns Walk, is that a 3 or a 5 Pud, I can't read her writing?" She handed the paper to DC Ambrose. "Yep, it's a 3, number 13, unlucky for some, eh?"

"Yes, thanks Pud, hopefully them and not us." Beth reached for the bell. She was just about to press it for the third time when she saw a figure through the patterned glass.

"Ang on, 'ang on, hold yer fuckin' 'orses, where's the pissing fire like, I'm not even...." Stacey stopped in her tracks, trying to focus on the cards being held in front of her face. "If any fucker 'as shopped me to Social Services, yer can check 'im right. Our Kyle's watching his videos, he's 'ad summat t'eat an all."

The girl was standing there in a faded pink t-shirt nightie, her hair tangled and creases in her young, blotchy skin, she'd obviously just got up.

"Stacey Lester, I'm DS Flynn, this is DC's Chapman and Ambrose, we are not here to do with Kyle, or yourself, we just want to know if Liam Dalby is here with you." Beth stepped forward to catch the girl as Stacey buckled slightly, she leant on the wall, turning a deathly shade of gray.

"I think I'm gonna be sick. Fuckin' ell, is he missin'? Oh god! This is all my fault! You berra' come in." She seemed genuinely worried as the officers squeezed into the tiny flat, past the filthy kitchen, the bedroom with a double bed and single bed squashed in the one room, clothes and toys strewn everywhere, then into the small grubby lounge.

Gazing up at them was a small cherubic boy, with a mass of black curls.

He was sitting on the floor, still in his stained pyjamas, it was now half twelve. Two empty crisp packets lay next to him and a half-eaten biscuit. His grubby face smiled, as the officers took in the sight. He held out his little hand, ingrained and dirty with black fingernails.

"Mammy up now, we can go mucky pub for crisps." Stacey tried to prise him away from the video, but he began to cry. "He's okay Stacey, DC Ambrose will keep young Kyle amused, won't you?" But Kyle was having none of it and rushed towards Beth, grabbing her round both legs.

"Sorry, he's not very good wi' men, he'll only go with us girls, or his dad, it's just the way he is." Beth sat down, pulling the small boy onto her knee. He instantly curled into her, his head under her chin. A surge of protectiveness soared through her whole body as she enveloped her arms round him, doing her best to ignore the smell from his unwashed body, she pretended she was looking over into her notebook.

"Okay, I think we might manage as we are, for the time being. Right, if I'm baby minding DC Ambrose better make us a cup of tea, is that okay Stacey?"

The girl had flopped heavily onto the settee, DC Chapman trying to avert his eyes at the already stretched T-shirt nightie, which covered very little. She sighed deeply lighting up a cigarette. "I'd rather 'av a strong coffee, it's all there, in t' tins. Liam gave me some extra shoppin' money this week…...Christ what 'ave I done..."

"I don't understand Stacey, what *have* you done? What do you think is your fault? What do you think has happened to Liam?"

"He had to pay off the money lender again. He said I had to stop spendin', stop going out so much and that……It's just I wanna be wi' me mates, I want clothes

168

and that. I don't wanna be stuck wi' *him* all the time." She points her cigarette in Kyle's direction. Kyle buries his head, as Beth holds his cold, grubby little body.

"But he's your son Stacey, he needs you, he's your responsibility. If you feel like that why don't you contact Social Services yourself?" Stacey leaned forward sharply, clearly vexed. "Oh, yeah, the bloody Dalbys would love that! Think they're the bloody Royal family that lot." Beth assumed she meant as in, Jim Royal etc. Surely, she didn't hold them in any higher esteem.

"If they had their way poor sod would have bin called, Count Kyle Dalby...   I mean, what the fuck's that all about. Liam's middle name is......Lord......They're crackers the fuckin' lot of 'em!"

Beth   interrupted   her   rant.   "But Liam….Lord….Dalby, can't be crackers can he Stacey? Otherwise, you wouldn't have had a 'relationship' with him   and   wouldn't   be allowing him to give you, amongst other things, a son, money for shopping and to pay off your debts......would you? By the way Stacey where are Kyle's sisters, your two other children?"

Stacey's face puckered. "You sure yer not from the social? They're round at me mams. The girls always go on a weekend. Me brother comes for Kyle around four. He reckons it's sissy for him to be with the girls all the time."

DC Ambrose plonks down a tray of mis-matched cups and a chipped mug, proffering Stacey a strong coffee.

"I thought you said he didn't like any males except Liam, his daddy."

Beth felt Kyle begin to shake as she held him. She now desperately wanted her ever faithful woman's intuition to be wrong, very wrong.

"Our Ste is okay. Kyle just makes a fuss 'cos his dad always spoils him. Tekin 'im t'seaside, park, zoos and that. Our Ste can only afford videos and some pop and that, so 'e as t'stay in like. He's just spoilt, a daddy's boy, aren't yer Kyle? Spoilt daddy's boy, eh?"

Beth held the small boy tightly, feeling in the pit of her stomach that this poor child was anything but spoilt. She now had another, important *'to do'* on her ever growing, 'to do' list.

"Well, though it pains me to say it Stacey, we're not here about Kyle, sadly. We want to know what you think has happened to Liam."

Stacey began to bite her bottom lip, obviously knowing she had to tell some semblance of the truth, so that the Police would maybe find him first. Let's face it, she needed his money, she couldn't manage just on benefits. Mind you if he was found dead, she could maybe get disability, for stress and that, she wouldn't be fit to 'work' at all then.

171

"I told him I'd paid the last lot of money he gave me to clear me debts, it was over a week late, he said if they added any more interest, he couldn't pay it. I was supposed to pay it Wednesday, but I went out. Well......me and me mates like, we went up the Metro Centre, for the day like."

"How much?"

"Four hundred and fifty quid."

Beth tried to stay calm. "You mean Liam gave you all that cash to pay off your money lender and you blew it *all* on one days shopping?"

Stacey's bottom lip dropped like a scolded child. Beth stared at this pathetic girl, not yet twenty, who had been having children since she was fourteen years old. She hadn't had a childhood, no fun teenage years with friends. So how could anyone expect her to be responsible, or to grow up. She hadn't because she didn't know how.

Stacey looked down at the floor. "I was gonna do a lost purse thing. All the lasses do it when they're short. Yer just go to the DSS, say you've lost yer purse and you'd just cashed yer giro like. Then yer just av t' get a Lost Property number from your lot at the front desk and the DSS pay yer money like, it would 'av kept 'em away another week." The officers sat looking incredulous.

"You mean the police are assisting benefit fraud?" DC Chapman's mouth moves open and shut taking on a goldfish like appearance.

"Well, you 'av to be careful which office yer go to like, some will do a couple of checks like, but yeah, I know loads who do it. Losing yer benefit books is good scam, not that I've ever done it. Someone told me.......but if I was desperate like."

Beth sighed. "Well, they do say, everyone else seems to be able to work the system better than us. Right, let's try this again Stacey, can you tell us when you last saw Liam?"

Stacey's expression changed again. "Thursday night. He was with that mongy cousin of 'is, Dabber. Gives me the bloody creeps 'e does. They were late, then Liam 'ad a go at me for spendin' an' that. I couldn't be bovvered with 'im, so I fucked off wi' me mate. I left 'im in the pub with that prick."

Beth looking skywards hearing her less than ladylike language in front of her child added. "Dabber being.....Dwayne...Prince...Dalby I presume. Can you remember the pub you left them in?"

"Yeah, it was 'Charlie's Bar' on Albert Road......okay?"

Beth felt the child in her arms relax and noticed he was sound asleep. Stacey had noticed too. "Huh, look at that, I can never get the bugger to sleep. I 'av to put 'is videos on till two int' mornin' just to shut him up. You gonna have t' wake 'im, Ste gets mad if he's hyper with him on a night like."

Beth carefully lifted the child turning and placing him, still asleep, on the warm chair she'd just left. "Stacey, he's not even three years old, he needs all the sleep he can get. Maybe if you read him a story instead of videos. Can't you see how the sound of our voices, just talking calmly sent him off."

"Well, if yer not from the social yer shud bloody well gerra job there. I know what 'e needs, I'm 'is mother, right. I thought you were trying to find Liam, that's what yer said."

"No actually, we're trying to find Dwayne Dalby, but if you think your money lender might be looking for Liam and he's at risk, the Police can assist you. I'll give you the number to ring and you can report him as, 'missing', okay?" Beth looks at her with authority.

175

"But, but....I told them he'd be paying the money, it's five hundred pounds now, they'll do him for that, he might be......fuckin' dead, don't you people fuckin' care......or what?"

"Stacey, had *you* cared about your family and Liam and had a little more self respect for yourself, surely you would have paid *your* debt already, with all the money Liam gave you and not gone shopping? Just out of interest who is your money lender, anyone we know?" Stacey's face puckered again in defiance.

"They don't exactly show their fuckin' ID do the'? All I know is they call 'im, Brickhead and the lad that comes for the money is called, Jed." She got up from the settee clearly annoyed at them trying to point some guilt her way. "Yer can see yer'sels out."

She stood there, trying to look angry, cigarette in one hand, the other on her hip, like a large pink teapot. The tortoise neck craning and as she puffed her chest out, her nipple rings protruding through the cheap fabric of the ridiculously short nightie, which had a slinky panther motif, stating the message, 'Let me get my paws on you.' It was a sight that both the male officers averted their eyes from, cringing as they left the flat, wishing to erase the vision from their eyes...

Beth wouldn't let it go till they reached the office. "What a clip, has she no shame! I mean…...nipple rings!........She's a mother of three young children......that was disgusting! Booze, ciggies and nipple rings, instead of food for your kids......jeeeez!"

"Beth, for God's sake! Will you stop! Please let me forget that vision in pink, it's lunch time, that sight has seriously affected my appetite, brrrrrugh" Chappie visibly shudders.

"I'll drop you off boys, I've got to pick up a suit from the dry cleaners and I'm just dropping Mr

Robinson's work keys off for him, I'll be back in half an hour, okay."

DC Chapman quickly opened his door again and leaned in.

"You're going to Harry Robinson's house, do you want someone with you?" Beth raised her eyebrows. "Not you as well Chappie, I'd have thought better of you, you know the facts."

DC Chapman looked a little guilty for momentarily doubting his DS, not just his DS, but a good friend. "Sorry, just with Pud saying there might have been two, you know, one doing the planning maybe......sorry."

"I'll be fine. I'm only dropping his keys off, he needs them for work on Monday, they were in the coat Kenny seized, can you believe it, he never even checked the pockets?" She grinned at him.

Chappie laughed loudly, backing off from the car. "Actually! I can believe that the big numb-nut! See you in thirty Beth."

Chapter 11

Beth parked on Linthorpe Road, picked up her suit, stretched her legs for ten minutes and grabbed a chicken wrap from Dachini's sandwich bar.

She eventually drove slowly up Essex Street, mentally counting to herself, 120, 122, 124. The terraced house was clean, the paint work was fresh, the door a lovely Royal blue.

It seemed a quiet road. A couple of doors were open, one elderly lady, some way down the road, out sweeping her step. A couple of lads tinkering with a car on the front, radio on, but she could only just hear it, just a nice quiet town road.

A group of Asian ladies passed, laughing and chatting in their own language. Made her wish she'd had time to take on the Hindi and Urdu classes that were on offer last year. At least she'd have been able to share the joke.

She knocked and waited, finally the door opened slowly, Mr Robinson peered out. "Can I help you madam." Beth was taken aback at his gentle politeness. "Hello, Harold Robinson? I'm DS Flynn, Middlesbrough CID, we met momentarily at the scene and I spoke to you on the phone." She quickly showed her ID card.

"I am so sorry, very ignorant of me, I was expecting a man, shouldn't in this day and age. Do forgive me, I'm a bit old fashioned. Not that I don't think women aren't fully capable. Mrs Reed down the road drove tanks in World War II. My mum and I did all the DIY together, strong as an ox she was....till... sorry...I'm rambling...."

"Don't apologise Mr Robinson, it was...well, almost a man, that dealt with you last time. DS Radford is busy at present, on other actions. I was in the area and wanted to get your keys back to you for Monday."

Harry opened the door fully. He was a big man, broad shoulders, a little unkempt, but that could be due to the upset of the last couple of days. Beth felt he lacked a woman's touch. He looked older than his 48years. He smelt strongly of coal tar soap. Reminded her so much of her gran. Every time Beth stayed with her, she'd always open up a new packet of Wright's coal tar soap.

Harry broke her thoughts.

"I'm sorry, forgive my manners, leaving you standing on the doorstep, please come in, would you like a cup of tea DS Flynn, the kettles always on here. Mum always used to say I'd end up with a tea-belly instead of a beer-belly. Sorry, you're probably too busy to...."

"Nonsense, it's probably very unladylike, but I have the fine starts of a tea-belly myself and would love a cuppa. I can't be too long though, my officers are awaiting my return to continue our investigations."

She pictured them...hard at work? Chappie and Pud, feet up on her desk, chip grease on her paperwork, stuffing their faces. She smiled to herself.

"Make mine a strong one please, no sugar thanks."

Harry directed her into an immaculate, compact, front room, his mum probably called it the front parlour, her gran always did. Only for best, for special visitors, like the Doctor, or the funeral Director, or Police, seen as respected human beings, with respected professions. Beth felt herself take a deep breath. Well at least there was still some left who felt that way.

Harry reappeared several minutes later with a lovely decorative tray, china cups and saucers and a small plate of biscuits. "Mum always said, ladies should always drink from china cups." She saw him smile for the first time, as he lowered the tray down and turned his head towards a photograph taking pride of place. Smiling back out at him was a sweet old lady, with a real twinkle in her eye, snowy white hair in a Royal blue dress with a dainty string of pearls round her neck.

"Do you feel as if she's never left? Must bring you comfort to look at that photo and see her so happy." Harry tilted his head slightly, in thought, as he poured the tea.

"I have moved on you know, I do know she's gone, I don't live as if she's still here or anything." He looked straight at Beth with a terrible, betrayed sadness that stabbed her in the pit of her stomach.

"That's not why I'm here Harry. You were questioned and released at the station by DS Radford, you were *his* suspect, not mine. You can talk to me about anything and I mean anything, that's why I'm here. Talk to me about the weather if you like......or.....or this gorgeous cat of yours." Beth mentally thanked the huge feline specimen that came waddling through the doorway on cue.

Harry laughed at this point. "This is Billy, he was mum's, he's latched onto me now, cupboard love of course." His big hands chucked the chin of the large cat, who in return head-butted his leg and began to rumble with a loud purr, gazing up at him. Harry quickly patted his knees and the large lump of a cat, with amazing ease, leapt deftly onto his lap, pummelling him gently as Harry stroked his back.

Beth smiled. "Well, you two are certainly a match made in heaven."

Harry carefully lifted his cup over the cat's large head and took a sip of tea. "Not quite the same as human company though. It does get lonely sometimes. That's why I feel for all these elderly people, on their own. That's why I visit, help and chat. I'm no weirdo, like that DS Radford implied. I often sit here thinking. What if I never find anyone, what if I'm just here on my own, for the next thirty odd years? It's like being widowed without having the marriage first." Beth saw the deep sadness in his eyes.

Beth desperately tried to think of some positives.

"If you go out and about with work so much, you must meet plenty of people. The elderly you help, they may have daughters, granddaughters, nieces......do you go anywhere in the evenings?"

He sighed. "I pop round the corner and have a half pint with my work buddies, you know, on Crescent Road. That's only on a Monday though. I do the Bingo at the Sycamore Nursing home on a Wednesday. But some of the care assistants there are a bit young, bit silly. My nickname is 'Jolly Green Giant', so you can imagine what they're thinking." Beth looks straight at him and smiles.

"Ah, the immaturity of youth. I can remember when I was in my twenties, thinking once you reached your thirties you may as well pack up your hormones. Forget romance and invest in a good set of thermals and furry slippers. How wrong I was, I wouldn't be twenty again for all the......Yorkshire Tea in England."

Harry laughed again. "A tea connoisseur, I'm impressed. Jilly hated tea, she drank nothing but strong black coffee, horrible stuff, she hated china cups too. She used those things that looked like soup bowls with a handle......" He stopped sipping his tea again, a faraway look in his eyes.

"Jilly? A girlfriend of yours?"

"Was...... my...fiancée, till mum got ill, I moved back here to help her. Not Jilly's fault, she had young parents doing their own thing. She wasn't close to her family. She couldn't understand the bond....it was difficult...for everyone."

Beth didn't want to leave Harry on maudlin thoughts.

"I'm a firm believer that there is someone out there for everyone, you just have to be in the right place at the right time......and on that note Mr Robinson, I'm afraid my right place at this particular time should be my office. Thank you so much for the tea, made a world of difference to the grey canteen stuff in a plastic cup I can tell you. You take care of yourself......and don't worry. We will find out who did this to Mrs Linton....I promise."

Harry stood up, Billy gently rolled off his knee reluctantly, knowing it was a rare occurrence to get onto the best sofa. But Harry didn't seem to notice, his eyes visibly watering.

"I wish he'd been there when I arrived, I wouldn't have been responsible for my actions, but he wouldn't get the chance to lounge in prison at the taxpayers' expense, that's for sure." He quickly checked his anger. "I'm so sorry, I shouldn't vent my spleen in front of you, but it just seems so wrong."

Beth put her hand on his arm. "I know what you're saying, but I'd rather that low-life was lounging in prison than someone, as caring and decent as you, was doing time at *his* expense."

"Thank you for getting my keys back DS Flynn, I know you'll do your best for Mrs Linton, I know you'll do your best to find him and make sure he gets what he deserves." If only, thought Beth...if only.

She walked back into the office, slinging her jacket onto the back of her chair, she could see the look of concern on Chappie's face. "You okay Beth? You look a bit drawn, any problems there?" Beth clicked on her computer, gathered her notes and pens together. "I don't have any doubts concerning Mr Robinson, in fact if we had more Harry Robinsons in this world, it'd be a better place."

"Hey, you be careful there Beth, don't let the charm and old-fashioned soft soap fool you. Why do you think he's on his own at his age? He'll have some weird fetish, frightened anyone normal off, now he's left sniffing round old ladies. You're an intelligent woman Beth, surely you're not taken in by him."

Beth turned and glared at Kenny Radford as he sat back in his chair, his legs apart, his arms stretched up behind his head, with that look on his face.

"That's not like you Kenny. Sticking to the one and only suspect like glue. Never known you stay with the first thing that comes along, that's not your natural bent is it? What's your fetish then? Look at you, aren't you a mere 41 years old, divorced......on your own.......all alone......?"

Kenny swung his legs round and got up briskly, grabbing a radio and his pocket-book. "Well at least I'm happily divorced...at least I've had a normal relationship at some point in my life." He looked like a spoilt child going to sulk as he headed towards the door.

Then added. "Huh! And your post-divorce life is hardly one social whirl. You're hardly beating the blokes off with a stick! You're just a gym bunny with her pooch for company." Beth smiled, the words coming out of a big, sulky boy rushing away in case she retaliated. "Well, thanks for noticing I work out Kenny....maybe it's the calves…...or have you been checking out me biceps?"

Kenny strode out of the room. Chappie and Pud were sniggering behind their computers. "He was blushing there Beth; did you see his face? You're not going to let him get to you on this are you?"

"No way…....even if he is right....he's got to work damn hard for a result." Chappie leaned towards Beth, wheeling his chair across. "I thought you said……. did something happen? What happened Beth?"

"Nothing! I still don't think it's Harry Robinson, but I was proved wrong once before, I'll take nothing for granted. Forensic results, that's what we need. Let's get some paperwork done over the next day or so. Make some phone calls, gather some intelligence, then we'll make a move Monday."

"We need a name to the fingerprint on that outside light, possible DNA on the milk carton and a name to the.... 'man in black'."

Beth could see Chappie champing at the bit from the corner of her eye.   "Oh! Just get it over with will you."

Chappie, like an over excited child eagerly obliged. "Batman! Errr....Johnny Cash...Dracula......the Milk Tray Man?......."

Beth smiled and sighed loudly.

Chapter 12

"Fuckin' hell." Dabber muttered crossly as he crawled from the grubby bedding. He lit a cigarette and pulled on his tracky bottoms and slowly descended the stairs. He knew he would have to go to court today. He had outstanding fines and a street robbery to take into consideration. If he didn't make this quick appearance, they'd come looking for him on a bench warrant, he didn't want the attention, or questioning, that's the last thing he needed. His solicitor would get him straight in and out, no fuss.

There'd be that many in there on a Monday, place would be heaving, they wouldn't hang about. He'd risk it.

"Shell darl, couldn't put us up a quick bacon sarnie could yer?"

Shelly had decided that she wasn't getting much out of this deal anymore. Both men had spent the last three days either pissed as farts, or high as kites. She was pig sick of cleaning up after them, hiding the drugs away in case of an intrusion. Making tea and food for them and others that arrived every few hours, that's if they could stay conscious enough to eat, between drink and drug stupors.

Neither of them had given her anywhere near a good session. Kieron had managed a drunken grope and

Dwayne had all the moves, just a shame they were at the speed of light!

She tutted at the sight of his scrawny body, as he tried to wrestle on a pair of Kieron's socks.

"Shouldn't you be going back to Liam's for your clothes and that, Dwayne? Yer' Auntie Mim'll be worried, won't she?" Dabber sucked his teeth. "What the fuck do they care! Anyway, I won't be in yer way, I'm at court at......I think it's ten, could be eleven...I'll go round me solicitors first anyhow. Then I'll 'ave to try and get some more cash."

Shelly tried to smile at this. "Are you gonna pay us a bit for staying here then?" He looked at her like she was mad. "Am I fuck! Kizza's a mate, he doesn't want me t' pay nout to stay here, you ask 'im. I paid for the drink, snout and that, we're good. Anyway, I'm off now. Might see ya later babe, if yer lucky."

Shelly sighed heavily, knowing it would have to be another day of selling what she could get shoplifting. Maybe she'd just nip round to Jean's. Jean says she'd get her work over the factory. Kieron didn't want her working, says it'll affect the benefits. More like it'll mean he might have to get up off his drugged-up backside and find work too. Work...it was like a bloody swear word in this house. Well, she was fed-up living on handouts, on the never never, looking over her shoulder. She still had *some* pride, somewhere.

She spent her days defrauding catalogues, shoplifting, wearing dodgy fakes. In and out of the courts, then hassled by people who'd bought the stuff, threatened for money by Milo, having to do them favours when Kieron couldn't pay up for drugs. She was bloody fed-up of it all. She the hood up of her gold padded bomber jacket and walked quickly through the estate towards Jean's house.

Dwayne Dalby barged into the solicitor's office on Albert Road, talking loudly as he past the elderly couple who were standing at the counter with the receptionist.

"Oi! Mr Pallent's with me for court this mornin', is he in like?"

The receptionist apologised to the couple as they backed away from the counter. She looked at him patiently, raising an eyebrow, obviously well used to, the majority of her partners clients.

"Good morning Mr Dalby, if you would like to take a seat, I shall let   Mr Pallent know you're here." But he didn't sit down, he lit a cigarette and went outside, then came back in, pacing the waiting area, flicking the large palm plant leaves impatiently.

A door finally opened. "Ah, Mr Dalby, do come in.

Mr Pallent gestured from the door into his office with a slow swing of the arm. "I'll just go over the details with you, should be quite straightforward this morning, have you done and dusted in a jiffy."

"What the fuck you on about, they did the fingerprintin' and that at the station before like." The solicitor still kept his air. "Do come into the office Mr Dalby." He looked towards the ceiling, then towards the receptionist, who smiled politely, as he shut the door.

The Teesside Magistrates courts were a hive of activity as they climbed the steps and walked through the huge glass doors. Mr Pallent shuffled his papers as he walked towards the security desk. "We're here for 10.45, Dwayne Dalby."

One security man checked Dabber over, as the other checked and ticked the large open book on the table. Mr Pallent headed towards the boards to check which courtroom they were in.

Just as Dabber was about to follow, the second security man spoke.   "Excuse me, Mr Dalby, there's a letter been left here for you."

He turned back, looking puzzled. A bloody letter, he swore under his breath, snatching it from the Security guard, hoping it wasn't another summons. He shuffled from one foot to the other. What if it *was* another summons, what if it was from Nottingham. Shit, shit, but if he didn't take it, the solicitor would. He didn't want him to see it. He took the small white envelope and stuffed it in his pocket.

"Anything we should be reading now Mr Dalby? Mind you, white envelopes aren't normally a worry. It's those nice brown ones that should worry you."

Dabber shuffled his feet. "Talking of brown ones Mr Pallent, I'm just off t'bogs okay?"

Mr Pallent winced slightly. "Yes, right. Well, we're in court 17, we'll have to have another quick run through just before we go in okay, don't be too long Mr Dalby?"

"Yeah, right, keep yer poncy wig on mate, I'll be with you in five."

Dabber rushed through the door, into a cubicle and sat down quickly tearing open the envelope. His heart pounding, there was no way he was going down for that now. He struggled to read the writing, not because it was poor, but because he'd rarely spent a full week at school after the age of nine and even the previous years at a school desk had passed him by.

He hated school and several teachers had tried to explain how difficult life would be without the ability to read and write well. What did they know, boring fuckers, he'd never had a problem in a dole office, or a police custody suite, they read everything out to you, several times. Filled all the forms in, wrote everything up for you. All he had to do was sign his name. He didn't need to read a book to further his knowledge. He knew the system inside out. He'd had a long apprenticeship and was now a master criminal. He laughed to himself. "Huh, what the fuck do they know." He scoffed under his breath.

It was a bloody note from Liam, thank fuck for that. Trust him to remember me court date, silly sod. He managed slowly silently, staring at a couple of words and cursing till the words came to back to him and he got the jist of the note.

'Dwayne, I rang Stacey to speak to Kyle......I know she still owes money. I don't want her to know where I am. Meet me near the 'workies' on Union Street at 10pm. I've got money, I want you to pay Brickhead off.

Good luck at court mate, Liam.'

Fuck, what a stroke of luck. Wonder how much. Should be able to take a wedge out without causing any probs....sorted. Dabber stuffed the envelope into his pocket and swaggered out of the Gents. That was his cash problem out the way. He climbed the stairs, his eyes searching for Mr Pallent. This would be a bloody doddle.

Just over an hour later, the swagger was back as Dabber emerged from the Courts and into the sunshine. "Well, Mr Dalby, adjourned till a later date, good job I mentioned that witness, that should keep them busy for a while. You are going to have to pay the two fines though. Not bad going though, only £70 a piece and you'll be paying that out of your benefits at £3 a week. You should be happy with that Mr Dalby?"

Mr Pallent looked at his watch, 10 to 12, he could squeeze a lunchtime

202

expenses on the top of this one. The Legal Aid system was a boon. It did mean a lot more trainees, jumping on the legal gravy trains and work was becoming very competitive, but God Bless the Americans and their Litigation teams, now they were in full swing. Money to be made on each and every corner, especially if it's a corner with dodgy paving. He smiled to himself.

"Yeah, blob on Tim mate, see ya."

The solicitor gritted his teeth, he hated having to get on first name terms with this sort, but they were the money-machine of his world. He got used to it quickly. A few hours a day then into his Lotus and back home to a lifestyle and a world away from this. Ironic that the crap at the bottom of the barrel, gave him the means to be the cream at the top.

Just as Dabber was about to go off in the opposite direction, the solicitor saw three CID officers approaching them. It was obvious Mr

Dalby assumed they were colleagues of his and didn't recognise them as plain clothed police officers. DS Flynn smiled at Mr Pallent, as DC Chapman and DC Ambrose stepped a little behind Dwayne Dalby.

She then turned to face him, her back to Mr Pallent. "Dwayne Prince Dalby, we would like you to accompany us to the station. We would like to ask about your whereabouts on the evening of Thursday 16th February into the early morning of Friday 17th February 1993."

Dabber turned on Mr Pallent. "This your fuckin' doing is it?"

Mr Pallent, looked down at him, staying ever calm. "Mr Dalby had these officers asked me for you to attend the station this morning, I would have taken you there myself. It's next door for heaven's sake, why would I have just concluded our conversation." Dabber stared at him blankly. "Mr Dalby, would you like me to come with you? I feel it may be possibly beneficial if I was with you in interview."

Dabber sniffed. "Fuckin' too right mate. They're not pinning 'out on me. Y'know what they're like." Dabber was taken across into the station and into an interview room. He strode cockily across the room before looking over at Beth.

"Strong coffee, two sugars darl, yer couldn't get us an ashtray an all could yer, I'm gaspin' for a fag."

Chappie shot across the room like a whippet, Beth had never seen him move so fast, he put his face six inches from Dabbers. "You will address this lady as, DS Flynn and a PC will get you a coffee and an ashtray, as soon as they have time, is that clear Mr Dalby."

Dabber lit up anyway, taking a long deep drag of his cigarette he leaned back into the chair slowly and stared at DS Flynn. Mr Pallent pulled his chair up to the desk, opening his briefcase, he took out a pad and pen. "Well, DS Flynn and what is it you would like to ask my client?"

Beth nodded her head and DC Chapman clicked on the tape machine. "Interview with Dwayne Prince Dalby commencing at 12.25pm, Monday 20th February 1993, in the presence of his solicitor Mr Timothy Pallent. Officers present, myself DS Flynn, along with DC Chapman."

"As we said outside Dwayne, we'd like to ask you a couple of questions about Thursday and Friday of last week. Firstly, could you tell us where you were on that Thursday evening, that would be Thursday 16th February 1993?"

Dabber tilted his head slightly, looked at the wall, thought carefully, then returned to stare straight at Beth. "No comment."

"Dwayne...we have already spoken to your Aunt, Miriam Dalby and Uncle, Earl Windsor Dalby, so we know that you had, apparently, gone into the town with their son, your cousin, Liam Lord Dalby, is this correct?"

"What yer fuckin askin' for, if yer already know then?" His tongue ran round the front inside his bottom lip as he sucked his teeth.

"Is that a yes Dwayne? Is...... 'into town' Middlesbrough town centre?"

"Yep."

"Did you and Liam meet anyone while you were there?"

"No comment."

"We have it from Liam's girlfriend Stacey Lester, that you met her and a friend there, but you didn't stay with them long. Is this correct?"

Dabber looked bored. "Look if you already know everything, why don't you just tell me what I'm supposed to have fuckin' seen, or done, right...."

There was a knock on the door. DC Chapman opened it.

"For the tape PC Wilson is entering the room with an ashtray and a cup of coffee for Mr Dalby." The door was closed again.

Beth persevered. "Stacey has told us that you left Charlie's bar at around 11.20pm. We also have intelligence from two uniform police officers that you were causing a bit of a disturbance in a Kebab shop on Borough Road around 11.40pm, you then left when the officers arrived and you then headed off towards Union Street. We'd like to know where you went after that."

Dabber slurped the hot coffee noisily, getting into his stride.

"So would I....... I was prob'ly fuckin' mortal by then." He knew what to say and what not to, he was good, they'd get nothing on him. He smirked.

"You're saying you were under the influence of alcohol, so much so, that you didn't know where you were, or what you may have done?"

"Hey! Hold on Mrs, I said I was mortal, I wasn't that bad."

"Where did you go Dwayne? Neither you, nor Liam, returned home that night. We also have that information from your Aunt Miriam."

"Naw, well, right...our Liam's gone...he went off to......" Dabber stopped himself quickly. If he said something about the job Liam was doing they might find him, if they find him, he might not get his hands on that cash.

"Where has Liam gone Dwayne? Has anything happened to him? We need to trace Liam?" Dabber looked puzzled, what were they on about, were they just trying to find Liam? Bloody brilliant and here he was shit scared they might be after him for the break at that old bird's house, he was walking out of here no bother.

"No, right. He and Stacey 'ad a row like. She's always flirtin' round other blokes. He just fucked off to a mate's house, for a couple of days, no probs."

He flicked his ash nonchalantly and swallowed down the rest of his coffee, giving a pleased sideways glance to his solicitor.

"And the name of Liam's mate he may be staying with?"

"How should I know, he's got loads, I'm not his fuckin mother, why should he tell me where he's staying."

"So, Dwayne, after Liam left, where did *you* go?"

"I went off to a mate's house an 'all. I knew I couldn't go back to Earl's without Liam, Earl would reckon I'd got 'im into trouble, he'd fuckin lamp me."

"And can you give us the name of the mate you stayed with?"

"Yeah, me mate, Kizza…... Okay?!

"We will obviously have to check this story out, can you give us Kizza's full name and address please." Dabber put things in order in his own mind. Kizza and Shell knew nothing, he'd said nothing to anyone since that night...

"Yep, Kieron and Shelly Parker, Central Avenue, Whinney Banks, number......29 I think. Is that it then, love, can I go now?"

Beth leaned back staring at his hand, his yellow fingers stretching out to stub out his cigarette, the exposed spider tattoo, just crawling from under his sleeve. She shuddered....... She hated spiders.

"Interview with Dwayne Prince Dalby terminated at 13.21pm. Thank you for your time and co-operation Mr Dalby. We may have to speak to you again at some point, so don't leave the country."

Chapter 13

Mondays were bad enough, but Malcolm couldn't

for the life of him understand why Harry had come in

today. He looked rough. Ken had told him to take a few days off, but Harry wouldn't hear of it, he had a job to do.

"Harry, you okay mate?" They'd almost finished their shift and Harry was just locking up the last alley gate.

"Mal, you've asked me that at least ten times this morning. Honestly, I'm fine. If I could turn the clock back, I would, but you know that's impossible. If I could find the bastard responsible and not do time for giving him his just desserts, I would. I also know that's impossible too.... So, what will be will be...... I'm fine." Harry walked slowly back to the wagon with Malcolm.

Malcolm knew Harry well. He knew he must be upset, frustrated and angry. He was such a gentle giant and a good soul, they rarely heard him swear, or lose his temper. This must be just eating him up inside.

"Are you coming round the pub tonight, couple of jars might help mate." Harry had always known drink was

214

not the answer. It may help you forget for a few hours, but the same awful facts were still there in the morning....and you had a bad head to go with it!

He knew that wasn't his favourite cure, after a full week of it when Jilly left.

He had come back home that Friday night and seen his mum's face, pale, stained with tears. 'This is my fault isn't it Harry, for being ill.' It hit him so hard. He'd knelt down in front of her, his big bulk crumbling with the drink and the emotional punch of her words. He'd held her tight and they'd both sobbed long into the night. He had spent the rest of the hours till morning, drinking strong tea and wishing the hands on the mantle clock could turn back the other way........

Drink never solved anything, but his friends had helped. Malcolm had always been there for him, along with his wife, Karen, who was always baking and had always *just* happened to have made, two extra of everything and they always *just* happened to be passing his house, even though they lived over in Marton. He smiled to himself.

"I'll probably pop in for a jar Mal, you know me, creature of habit. I'll have me usual half bitter, then make me way round the darts and dominoes. You can't say I don't know how to party can you?"

Malcolm slapped his mate on the back and laughed. "Hey, I'll see if our Karen can ask that lass she works with to come along. You know, Carolyn. I think she's partial to a sherry and a game of dominoes."

Harry stopped suddenly. "Sherry, that's an old lady's drink. What you trying to say, I like old ladies? Are you thinking what the rest are thinking are you? Not you as well Malcolm...*you* don't think...."

Malcolm was shocked at Harrys reaction, but knew what the police thought.

"Harry, mate, for Christ's sake, what do you take me for? Sherry and lemonade in a half glass, it's all the rage apparently. I told you before about Carolyn, she's only thirty-nine, mate. You remember, broken engagement like you. You thought it was too soon before and I said I'd leave it for a while. Come on Harry, it has been a while now, I was just trying to help?"

Harry closed his eyes and sighed heavily. "I am so sorry mate, it's just...well, you know...all this going on.... and they think..." Malcolm opened the cab door and they climbed into their seats, in silence.

Back at the yard, they both finished their cleaning and paperwork. Harry saw Malcolm walking towards his car, as he wheeled his bike out of the work shed.

"Hey, Mal, maybe if Karen could sort something for next Monday? I would appreciate it, thanks. I'll see you and the lads tonight though. I think throwing something at a dartboard would help me more at the moment.......okay?"

Malcolm grinned over. "As long as it's not me you're throwing mate, see you later buddy." Harry waved as he peddled off towards Sainsbury's. His mum hated him using big supermarkets, but well, tonight he just wanted a ready cooked chicken, some microwave chips, tinned peas and an hour in the bath. Sorry mum, he could feel her tutting her disapproval, but smiled as he thought of Bobby making the most of sharing the ready cooked treat.

As he balanced his carrier bags carefully on each handlebar he cycled across town, over the junction and the traffic lights, he noticed out of the corner of his eye a dark blue car travelling close. He turned into Union Street, which was a 'no right turn' to vehicles, the car stayed with him. He pulled over, just about to check the number, when it pulled up so close to him, his leg was almost trapped between it and his bike. He had to lean into the pavement to see the occupants as the window opened.

"Oh, Mr Harold Robinson, been doing a bit of, 'help the aged' shopping have we?" Harry bristled as he saw the look on DS Radford's face and the smirking expression of his sidekick.

"If you class forty-eight as old Sergeant, then yes, this shopping is mine." Kenny Radford was not going to let it go. "Not visited any, confused old biddies today then? Not been getting, 'friendly' with some crazy old cat-lady then? You know what they say about paedophiles befriending single mothers to get at the kids. Which do you prefer, the cats, or the oldies?" Even DC Felling felt a little uncomfortable at his Sergeants comments and turned his head from Mr Robinson, squared his jaw, looking straight ahead at the dash.

But Harry was looking straight at DS Radford. He was getting fed-up of this officer's insinuations. He had always respected the police and knew, no matter how carefully picked, there was always going to be at least one bad apple in every barrel.

"DS Radford, you have every right to check my movements, if you feel I am still a suspect, but I would ask you politely, if you could save your comments for the taped interview you can have with me, when you have the evidence to prove I committed a crime. I know how frustrating it must be to not be the officer to nail the perpetrator of such an abhorrent crime, but if you keep tailing me, you're going to be last to find him. Sorry to disappoint you, Sergeant."

DS Radford then bristled in return. "We'll see about that Robinson. You just watch your back." With that he put his foot down and took off down the road, the tyres screeching. Harry's heart pounding from the confrontation, he slowly wobbled away from the kerb and made his way home.

Still upset from the words of DS Radford earlier, he hadn't enjoyed his dinner. He clicked on the kettle, scraped the chicken bones from his plate to the bin. Putting his plate into the sink, he ducked his head through the doorway to the downstairs bathroom, turning on the tap he stared into the mirror in front.

He wasn't going to be filled with self-pity, but he couldn't understand why people saw him so differently to what he saw himself. How could someone see helping the elderly as a perversion? How could someone put such an evil slant on caring for your own mother, for loving her? Didn't everyone love their own mum, enough to help them in loneliness and ill health? Why had it been questioned that her own son had returned to care for her, it filled him with overwhelming sadness.

"DS Radford." He could feel himself spitting the words. "The man has no insight, not an ounce of compassion." He held the sink sides and gritted his teeth.

It wasn't just Radford though was it. What about the girls at the home, calling him 'Jolly Green Giant', that wasn't a term of endearment was it? They were mocking him. A couple of them were even quite flirty with him. But he knew it was to watch him feel awkward, watch him go the colour of beetroot'. Just for a laugh, at his expense. His hair was neat, greying at the temples. Yes, he was tall, big, broad, but not ugly, not odd. He consciously flattened his hand down over his head.

Jilly never said anything detrimental about his looks. Previous girlfriends had never mentioned it. No one had gone screaming from a date. No, he was and never would be a monster, by a long stretch of the imagination.

He put his work clothing into the laundry basket walking back through to the kitchen in his boxers. Making a large mug of tea he went back through to the bathroom closing the door out of habit. He then lowered himself into the hot water, breathing deeply as the heat seared through to his bones. God, he loved that feeling after a cold day outside. As he sank deeper, he pressed the button for music from his little waterproof radio suctioned to the tiles nearby. Closing his eyes, he let the music and the heat of the water, take him away.........far, far away.

It was after nine, Harry zipped up his thick, padded coat against the cold night air, pulling up his collar he strode quickly up Crescent Road. He'd stayed in the bath longer than he'd meant to. Mal would think he'd said something wrong and wasn't coming. He quickened up his stride until, suddenly, out of nowhere, someone appeared round the corner of Kildare Street. Small and skinny, Harry's bulk nearly sent him flying.

"What the fuck are yer doin' yer big shit!"

Harry stared down at the thin, boned frame, in a navy tracksuit and cap,   pulled well down.

Dwayne looked up at the huge man standing in front of him, wondering if he should have lost it. Maybe get his knife ready, should he try and jump him first. No, this fucker could have a good shot, he didn't want a fight. Maybe he'd come this way another night, around the same time see if he were around. He'd like a go, fell a big shit like this, then rob the bastard. Doesn't look flash mind probably got nowt worth having. Rather have the guaranteed pay out from Liam tonight that's for sure.

Harry raised his hands. "Look, it was an accident, okay. You just appeared from nowhere." Harry was ready for him. His dad had shown him how to box when he was young, he'd also been in the territorials for a year, till he broke his arm. Not in combat but falling off his bike, but if this thing in front of him was going to try and rob him he would defend himself.......unless he had a gun, or a knife........

224

Dwayne began to walk away, towards Wicklow Street. "No worries, accidents 'appen mate, fuck it, no probs mate.......right." Harry didn't like the lads initial outburst, heightened and threatening. He kept taking a quick look over his shoulder, until he was safely inside the pub.

He'd no sooner walked in the door and he was handed a set of darts.

"Yeeeesssss! One hundred and eighty! Hey, Harry man, you're on top form tonight. Well focused bud...spot on!" Craig had seen his performance as he got the drinks in at the bar, carefully resting the tray down, he winked at the big man.

"Keep it up Harry, the ladies love a man who always hits the bulls-eye first time." Mal looked over at Harry, concerned he was still feeling a little sensitive on that front, from their conversation earlier. He was relieved to see Harry smile broadly.

225

"Well, you're the domino wiz Craig, what do *you* do for the ladies? Knock, knock, then fumble for a matching pair!" Everyone roared with laughter. Harry didn't really like being a crude bloke, but you had to hold your own with the lads. It was all banter. Truth be known, they were all soft touches at home with their partners and families.

Craig took it on the chin as they all sat down. "Someone's on fine form tonight, your darts playing obviously improves your sense of humour as well, big man." They grinned at each other as Mal sat down on the other side of Harry.

"Where's your Karen tonight then?" Harry asked taking a sip from his glass.

Malcolm shuffled a little on his seat. Harry caught his eye.

"Don't tell me, she's heard the news, not 100% sure of me now eh? Or has she and.... Carolyn is it?......discussed it all at work and now she won't be coming near me with a barge pole, next Monday....or any other Monday for that matter. Am I right?"

Mal looked more than a little hurt. "No! Bloody hell Harry man, me and Karen have been your friends for years. I know you're going through it, but you've got to trust someone. I was just a bit embarrassed to say…..she's baking again."

Harry looked puzzled. Mal leaned into him, so that only he could hear.

"She reckons you won't be eating properly, with the stress and the worry of losing your elderly friend and the police and that......I think we'll probably be, 'just passing' your place, around Thursday?"

Harry pulled his lips with his fingers trying to stifle a laugh. "Oh, Mal, I'm really sorry." Mal got in quick. "What for, not thinking we believed you, or for Karen's baking? You're going to have a freezer full! She's baking for England that woman, she's in the zone. I left her in a cloud of self-raising, shouting, 'don't slam the door you'll sink me sponges' plural! God help yer man!" Both men now laughed loudly.

Above the laughter Harry could just about hear someone, shouting his name, he turned. He could see Beryl behind the bar, clutching the phone receiver and waving. "It's for you Harry!"

His stomach lurched and his mind scrambled. Who could it be ringing him here, he hoped to God it wasn't the police again, could he not escape from that DS Radford, would they not give him a night off, he sighed as he reached the bar. Beryl passed him the phone, he tentatively put it to his ear. "Hello, this is Harry

Robinson." There was so much noise around him, he moved towards the corner of the bar, covering his other ear.

He heard someone clearing their throat and traffic in the background. "Harry…...Harry....it's me, Jilly. Please don't hang up, wouldn't blame you if you did mind. It's just that I read about that poor lady and you finding her. I'm so sorry about everything and I mean *everything.* I don't expect you to forgive me, but I feel bad walking out on you, when I did and when your mum was so ill."

Although he could barely hear her, Harry strained to catch every word, he could feel the knot in his stomach release. "Jilly, I'd never hang up on you. I know it was difficult for you too…...I know...I..."

"Harry, can you hear me? I'm on my mobile, I just pulled up at the side of the road. Impulse I guess....just felt I had to ring......I knew you'd be there on a Monday..... could we talk...could I

229

come to the pub....now maybe? I don't want you to feel under any pressure......we can just have a drink, you know....a chat...just catch up.......would that be okay? ......Harry?"

Harry felt a pang, his heart beat faster. She sounded different, softer, or was it just sympathy in her voice. Did she just feel sorry for him? No, that wasn't Jilly. Even when it had hurt like hell, she had been totally honest with him. She had never strung him along.

"Jilly, are you sure you want to walk in here, after all this time? If it's not a daunting prospect for you I'd be happy to see you, be good to catch up, I'll wait,   I'll just hang on here?"

The traffic noise got so loud and he could barely hear. "Thanks Harry, sorry about the noise. I'll see you soon okay. Bye......bye." Harry sighed, putting the receiver back slowly.

"Hey, big man! While you're catching flies at the bar you may as well get the last orders in, mine's a pint." Craig patted Harry's back as he headed for the gents.

"You okay Harry, who was that on the phone?" Harry balanced the tray of drinks and strode back over to the table, then leaned in towards Mal. "Keep it under your hat, but that was......Jilly. Can't quite believe it.... Jilly. Said she'll pop in here, said she'd heard about poor Mrs Linton, me being there.....I think she's just offering a shoulder."

Malcolm knew how much Harry had been hurt by Jilly walking out but knew he still cared for her very much. "So, a shoulder is enough then, after all this time? You'll want me to tell Carolyn to put her shoulders away then for now?"

Harry laughed, looking down at the floor, shuffling his feet like some bashful schoolboy. "Oh, I don't know Mal. I'm sure

Jilly has moved on easier and much further than me, it's been a good while now, she's just popping in for a drink and a chat....who knows....who knows."

Chapter 14

Dwayne had nipped in the offy for some tobacco and ciggy papers. He was hoping he could afford something a little better later. He walked slowly, peering into the shadows of Victoria Street, to see which 'girls' were out tonight. He jumped slightly as one stepped forward, into the light. He thought it might that old hag from the other night. God was she a mad fucker that one. He fancied a young one tonight. His eyes scoured Howard Street for Jade. Not to worry, he'd come back later when he had the cash.

He'd have to score as well. Milo's lads would be out and about. He could pay him what he owed, out of what Liam gave him. Liam was safe enough from Brickhead, working up there out the way. He couldn't give a flying fuck about Stacey. Liam's girlfriend, huh. She'd shag anything that would pay for her drink...... Maybe he should get a couple of bottles later, pay *her* a visit. He sniggered to himself, she liked him really, give her enough booze he could have her anyway. He could feel his groin ache, later, later. He had to get that cash first.

He stopped near the post-box on St Paul's Road, looked over towards the 'workies' club. Had Liam said near to, or outside? He wouldn't be inside, not with that lot of old farts, that's for sure. He saw several elderly men step out of the club. "Night George. Mind 'ow yer go me old lad."

They looked over towards the thin, shifty figure near the post-box. As one old fella with a stick began to shuffle slowly down St   Paul's, George called out.

"Bill, you be alright me old mucker, will you? Do you want me to get our Stan out, to walk you down home."

Bill waved his stick aloft, cheerily. "If someone wants to batter me senseless for two bob, I've 'ad enough alcohol to numb the pain."

Silly old tossers Dwayne thought. Just 'cos they wupped Hitler years ago, they think they're the bloody SAS! He crossed the road towards them. He could see them visibly trying to straighten up their hunched, old backs.

No way would they be intimidated by this low-life. What did he know about bravery, hard work, determination, blood, sweat and tears? They only had to look at the sloppy clothing and ape-like walk. No shirt or tie, no jacket, no polished shoes....no respect...no pride.

George and pals took in the pitiful sight. Look at him. He cared for nobody, he'd never learned how to. Not a partner, his parents, or even friends, but most of all he didn't care for himself. The men huddled together, shoulder to shoulder, hoping he'd just throw a punch, if he was armed...well...that might be a different matter.

"What the fuck's wrong with you lot like? Have any of you got a watch?   I don't want the fuckin' thing, I just want the time." Dabber had already noticed one of them quickly trying to remove his watch.

"It's just turned ten o'clock young man, are you waiting for someone in the club?" George said with obvious relief.

"Mind yer own fuckin business yer stupid old bastard, I only asked yer the time, nowt else, alright?" He could see the old man was clearly shocked, as were the others. He laughed at them walking past closely, sneering. He could hear them tutting, muttering the usual oldie crap... 'to think we won the war for that'... 'the country is going to the dogs '...yeah, yeah. Well, they'd all be fuckin' dead soon, Dabber thought to himself, snorting loudly.

Several others emerging from the club took a wide berth round him, or hailed a taxi hastily on seeing him obviously agitated, hopping from one foot to the other, his wild eyes staring at them from under his cap. Where the fuck was Liam? If he dobbed out on him now, there'd be fuckin hell to pay.

Then Dabber heard a loud whistle, he looked round, at first thinking someone was trying to hail a taxi. No one there, he turned the other way and caught sight of a dark figure in the shadows, just across the road, in Waverley Street.

"Liam! Liam! Fuck, is that you? About fuckin' time mate." He hopped, almost skipped across the road in excitement. He could see him backing towards the alley gate and into the shadows.

The anticipation was getting too much for Dabber. "Hang on mate, where yer goin'? Didn't think yer'd wanna be seen like, not with all that cash on yer, and Brickhead on yer case. How much av' yer got mate?" He reached his hand out greedily.

"Fuck it, what the......" Before he could utter another word, a hand fastened round his throat, turned him violently, twisting his arm up his back to breaking point to breaking point and he felt the metal mesh of the alley gate fall away in front of him. His skinny frame was dragged, as he struggled for release. His body was lifted forcibly from the ground and slammed heavily against the brick wall. The violent jolt shot his cap from his head, but this was quickly replaced by his hood, which was being pulled up and over his head to cover his face. "What the fuck you doin'...Liam....what the......"

Dabber tried a couple of moves, but his legs were quickly kicked from under him. He fell heavily onto his side, the pain rushing through his body. He struggled to his feet as punch after punch rained down on him. He fought with the assailant and his clothing, to free himself. "Shit! For fuck's sake...let me up......just let me get me fuckin' breath......" He finally managed to get a hand free, seizing the chance he quickly pulled a knife, slashing out, stabbing blindly into the darkness.

He heard a noise, like a groan, a whimper. "Yah! Got yer! Yer fucker! Where are yer........I'm gonna fuckin' kill yer now, make no mistake. No one gets the better of Dabber, yer......gonna fuckin' regret tekin' me on." As he tried to stabilise his footing, his ankle was grabbed and ripped from under him, the knife flew from his hand with a sharp clout to his wrist. His balance lost, he stumbled, sliding down against the alley wall, the rough brickwork sanding the skin from his face.

Now on all fours he made a desperate and final attempt to push himself up. Catching his breath, he felt an

239

almighty blow to the side of his head. He reeled backwards. The taste of blood filling his mouth, his eyes wide, as the pain seared through his head. He could feel his bowels go, then darkness as he fell forward, into a pile of rubbish bags.

"Oh bugger and I've just got me breakfast.......typical! An emergency briefing, not sure if that's a good sign, or bad." Chappie frowned at Pud. Beth looked through her paperwork.

"Have either of you seen the DI this morning? What's his mood like?"

"Couldn't tell you Sarg, not seen him. Midge told me about the briefing, SOCO had a message on their office board, first thing. You know old Wahay, if it's the 'right royal bollicking', he'll be in his office, pacing the floor for fifteen minutes before hand."

"Well, I just hope to God it's nothing our team has done, I really need to stay on this one, I've got to see this one through." Chappie raised an eyebrow. "Aha! Your runaway gravy train is gathering speed and away down that track, eh?"

Beth tutted loudly. "No.......I just really want this sick perv off the streets, we need him caught......although, as I said before, it will help with my, 'luxury break' pot for mum and dad. I've never been averse to a few extra hours and extra cash."

Chappie saw another chance to tease. "So, we'll all have a bit of extra cash to treat someone with then?" She stood up, flexing her aching fingers, then straightening her fitted skirt around her tall, willowy frame, while reaching for her jacket.

"You just keep your, 'luxury pot' to yourself Chappie, no one likes a show- off. Come on guys, our briefing beckons." Pud was laughing at Chappie, they both sniggered like a pair of naughty schoolboys who'd just looked up, 'penis' in the dictionary. Beth strode off down the corridor, shaking her head in despair.

DI Hayman did not look angry, but neither did he look that happy. His index finger and thumb were stroking at his moustache, as he waited for everyone to come into the incident room and get settled. He stepped forward and had a quick word with Phil Marsh and Sam Lawson, DI and DS from Technical Support Unit. Beth couldn't lip read, but presumed it was possible forensic results.

"Okey dokey......Ladies and gentlemen! Can I have your attention please. We have an important breakthrough, just hope some of our officers haven't sent our suspects running for cover."

DS Radford shot a look at Beth, then in a loud whisper, obviously meant for her ears. "See......told you it was Robinson. Another perv that needs taking off the streets.... permanently."

Beth gritted her teeth, she didn't even turn her head, just kept her eyes on the DI. He'd said suspects. Are they now assuming there is more than one.

"DI Marsh had a phone call from Wetherby labs this morning. They have a match for DNA, on the empty milk carton from Doris Linton's kitchen. The match is for one…...Dwayne Prince Dalby, a prolific burglar of this parish." The DI scanned the room till he spotted Beth.

"Did you not have Dalby in the interview room yesterday DS Flynn?"

Beth felt herself flush. Shit. This was just bloody typical. She could see Kenny out of the corner of her eye looking like a startled guppi.

243

"Yes, we did sir. We got him in for questioning after a court appearance, sir. We asked for his whereabouts during that time, in connection with a....'misper, sir. Liam Dalby, Dwayne's cousin, went missing on the same night."

The DI raised his eyebrows. "So, this, Liam Dalby, could be his accomplice? Or *he* could even be the attacker?" Beth was trying to gather her thoughts.

DC Chapman cut in. "Liam Dalby has no previous sir, we checked him out. Dwayne Dalby had an apparent alibi for the times given. DC Peel and DC Grant checked the address he stayed at that night, they said he was at their house from around 10 o'clock sir. We had no forensic, till now. How could we hold him? How could we have known any different before this evidence came to light sir?"

The DI stood thoughtfully, digesting the information, his mouth moving up and down, like a cow, chewing cud. "Right well,

I'll listen to the tape. May not be a bad thing. If he doesn't feel under any suspicion for this crime, he may even lead us to his accomplice. Remember, there is still that unaccounted fingerprint on the outside security light. I think we should get some obs on some addresses, check out his associates. Let's get every detail of his past. DC Chapman do you know where he moved from?"

Chappie reasonably prepared for any possible questions, deftly flicked through his notebook.

"City of Nottingham sir. Born there, most of his family are still living there sir. He came up here couple of years ago, to stay with his dad's brother, Earl Dalby."

The DI turned to have a quick word with an officer heading the Incident Room, who in turn quickly flicked through some papers and shook his head.

"No actions as yet for his profile......so....DC Chapman can you take that on? Beth has he got any other outstanding actions, is he free to head to Nottingham and see the family, old haunts etc.... can he take this one?"

Beth shuffled her papers, doing some quick thinking. "Er, yes sir, I'm sure we can try and manage without him." She quickly added. "Could I possibly have one of my team out of the incident room sir, for *our* continuing enquiries?"

The DI turned again to the officer who was now nodding.

"Yes, yes, absolutely. Right are we all clear on results needed today. Carefully does it, he is known to be violent. He has previous, for burglary and street robbery with menaces. He usually carries a knife, so be aware of that if searching him, also possible needles etc. He has a habit, so he needs a constant cash and drug supply. Shouldn't take too long to flush him out......human excrement will always float to the surface, eventually. Thank you everyone, have a good and productive day." Most people were heading for the door with their noses wrinkling.

"Not one of his best, 'be careful out there' speeches?" Chappie cringed.

"All that toilet talk, I'm going to have to leave you for ten minutes." As he turned to go, Beth grabbed his arm. "Thanks...... for pulling me out of the mire on that one."

Chappie laughed. "Don't you start with your dirty toilet metaphors as well. But just remember, when the shit hits the fan, I'm your man. Oh eh! I'm at it now!" He disappeared across the hallway.

Fifteen minutes later Chappie was at his desk ready for the off. He'd tidied himself up, quick squirt of expensive aftershave from his desk drawer, tie straightened, he grabbed his jacket and files.

"Sorry about this Sarg, DI just collared me in the corridor, wants me to take a pool car and a PC and go down to Nottingham now. See the officer that dealt with his previous. See if he's headed back down there......well, you know the score. Sorry to leave you high and dry......"

Beth slowly looked up from her paperwork. "Not at problem Chappie...honestly... hopefully it's just tying up loose ends until we have Dalby in custody. I'm glad the DI gave you the action, you're one of the best and you'll know what to do to get the *right* results......" She added with a smile. "But I shall miss you....well....the sight of your eggy ties....your innuendos....your..."

"Thanks Beth, I get the message.....love you too! I'll keep in radio contact, but you've got my mobile......" He then threw a set of keys onto the desk.

"Any chance of you feeding the moggies while I'm gone, I'll make it worth your while?" He winked at her and did a mock swagger from the office.

248

"You're incorrigible...you loon, go and get some police work done! What has Nottingham ever done to deserve you?!" Beth sighed heavily, lifting the next file, from an ever-growing tower on the corner of her desk as Chappie disappeared through the doors and downstairs to the yard.

Minutes later she heard a commotion. "Sarg! Sarg...you're not going to bloody believe this...Sarg!" Pud was striding down the corridor, waving a piece of paper at her. Beth looked up from perusing her numerous notes and witness statements. "After this last few days.......I'm not so sure....why what is it?"

"Our man in the 'long black coat'......he's been found. He rang the Incident Room, half an hour ago. WPC Taylor says he's come into Front Desk, she's put him in Interview Room 2. He's waiting to give a statement. What do you reckon Sarg?"

Beth stared straight ahead. "Well, we'd better get his statement then."

Beth stepped into the interview room and sat down. The male across the table from her wasn't quite what she'd expected. Even the worried frown and anxious look on his face did not detract from the strong features and warm blue eyes. He had a mid-brown mop of slightly unruly hair, but he was dressed impeccably. Mint green shirt, his tie, one shade darker. Unusual colour of suit, a soft hazelnut hue, beautifully made. She knew a classic suit when she saw one, her ex had bought many. Marc Jacobs possibly.......Armani? She was broken from her thoughts.

"I am really sorry for causing you problems in your investigations. My mother was unwell...and I thought I'd... I combine a visit with work...I never......"

Beth raised her hand. "Doris Linton was your mother?"

"No….no...sorry......Ivy Elliot is my mother." Beth was utterly confused.

WPC Taylor stepped forward with the notes she'd made when he'd arrived at the station Front Desk. "Right, okay then, let's just have a look here and start from the beginning. You are...Robert Finley Elliott?" She raised her eyebrows. He looked charmingly embarrassed.

"That's me. Finley was my Grandpa's name."

"Finley is pretty tame, I got, Shirley, as in Temple, one of mum's favourites as a girl." He smiled and the anxious frown subsided. Beth checked herself, just stay professional girl, this could be the assailant you're talking to gain their trust, don't get familiar.

"So.....Mr Elliott, apparently you seem to think you are the....'man in black' we've been searching for? Who was seen in Mrs Doris Linton's garden in the early hours of Wednesday 15th February 1993? Is that correct?"

Robert Elliott, put both, very well manicured hands onto the interview table, sliding them forward towards her. "If you take my fingerprints, I think you'll find they match prints you may have got from the lightbulb you took, from outside Mrs Linton's house." He leaned back again, sighing.

"My mother, Ivy Elliott, was a close friend of Doris. Mum just lives at the top of Maldon, number 91. She and Doris had spoken only a couple of days before......"

His anxious frown returned..... "Mum had been feeling unwell recently, I was coming up this way for a business meeting, possible client. I told mum I'd pop in to visit her. This was Tuesday...14th. We caught up, had a good old natter, but she had mentioned on at least two occasions, that poor Doris couldn't reach to change the bulb in her outside security light. Mum was worried she might fall if she couldn't   see her way properly."

His eyes flicked skywards. "Mum's a bit obsessive about safety and security. I'm glad in one way, better she's safe, especially with what happened, but she worries too much sometimes....they do at that age. Anyway, I was up with the lark on Wednesday, to get back to London for several appointments. It was still dark as I stepped out of mum's house and the security light came on. That's when I remembered.... Mrs Linton's light. I felt guilty I hadn't done it when mum mentioned it. I grabbed a couple of bulbs, hoping one would fit and rushed up the road to do, what I thought, was a good deed." He looked awkward and a little guilty.

"Mum was seen by a PC on Friday, but she hadn't realised I'd been and changed the bulb. She sobbed down the phone on Friday evening, telling me about poor Doris. I was stunned and felt dreadful for mum. By Monday's phone call she was worried sick, really frightened. She said that on the news and in the paper they

253

had spoken of a possible sighting, a 'man in black' seen nearby......and the assumption this may be a possible suspect. I suddenly realised...the 'man in black' could very possibly have been me..."

He reached under the table and held up a long, black mac from across his knees. "It's waterproof, I don't want to risk getting my suits ruined....they're expensive......I'm really very sorry. I came back up as soon as I could."

Beth sighed. "Well, by what you've told us Mr Elliott, you did what you could once you knew the facts. Obviously, we'll need a full statement from you, fingerprints and confirmation of your whereabouts at the times in question. Once we've checked your story out, you'll be eliminated from our enquiries. Thank you for coming in and saving us from anymore sightings and actions for......'the man in black'."

He looked apologetically at her. His eyes reminded her of Freddie's, when he'd just ripped apart yet another one of her best cushions......crinkled and appealing.

"There is a little way to go yet Mr Elliott, but hopefully the conclusions found will be the right ones for......everyone concerned." He looked a little puzzled but thanked the sergeant anyway.

Chapter 15

"Harry....weren't we over your way yesterday?
We locked all the gates...didn't we?" Harry looked up

from his sandwich box and shuffled round on the small, tea-room chair.

"Yes, we locked up...sure we did Mal...why, what's the problem?"

Mal perched himself on the edge of the table.

"Ken says we've got to nip over and check the gate on Warren Street alley. Apparently, Beany passed in his wagon, says it's open! Probably the bloody kids again, trying out stolen tools on the locks."

Harry reached for his coat, deftly picking out a chocolate mini roll, before closing the lid and tucking the sandwich box back into his rucksack. "Worth checking, we can pop a chain and padlock on, if they've broken the lock again. C'mon, it'll only take us ten minutes."

They borrowed the works old Leyland pick-up. Minutes later they turned into Warren Street from Princes Road. As Mal pulled up, it was obvious the gate was open, the gate was pushed back at least a foot. "Little buggers eh...we only collected yesterday, not as if there'd be much of 'out to nick........just extra hassle for us."

Mal turned the van round near the 'no through road sign' and pulled up. As Harry picked up the chain and padlock from the dash, Mal jumped out quickly to inspect the lock.

"It's not damaged Harry....not a bleedin' mark on it mate." Mal looked from one side to the other as Harry joined him. "How have they managed that? Was it you or me that locked this one?"

Malcolm stared straight ahead, thinking.... "Odds...evens, I did Wentworth, you did, Waverly, then Manor...I think Jeff was off the wagon...Oh! Oh God! Holy mother of...... hell!"

Harry watched as Mal's face turned a pale shade of grey. "Hey...mate...   Jeff will be okay, it's hardly a sackable offence Mal."

"No.....Harry....look!"   Harry   followed   the direction of Mal's finger as he pointed down the alleyway. There, sticking out from behind several rubbish bags, was a bloodied leg. Harry keeled slightly, swallowing hard as he felt his stomach begin to churn......surely it wasn't....

"Come on Mal, let's get a grip, it'll be some alchy, a tramp, druggie, got three sheets to the wind, lost their way, tripped over the rubbish in the dark, they'll be out for the count, slipped in here to sleep it off......you'll see." Harry wasn't sure who he was trying to convince, Mal, or himself.

They walked towards the pile of rubbish, not enough bags there to hide much. They'd only just cleared the alley yesterday, four black bags at most. They could see both legs now and assumed it was male, as the head was obscured by a bin-bag, clothing and dried blood. Mal truly didn't want Harry to see this, but he knew he couldn't cope with it alone. "Oh shit, Harry mate... dear god I'm sorry, you shouldn't have to...not after last week...is he...you know...?"

Harry braced himself and with the very tips of his finger and thumb reached down to check for a pulse. He steeled himself, to stop the rising nausea, as he touched the cold, bloodied flesh. "We'd better call someone Mal....yeah, I'm sure he's dead."

Harry and Mal sat in the van in stunned silence, as sirens wailed around them. Paramedics, police, one vehicle, after another. Finally, the door of their van was opened.

"Hello gents...DC Scott, Middlesbrough CID, I believe you found the body, would you mind just giving me a quick synopsis of the circumstances."

They stared at him blankly, trying to gather their thoughts.

"I realise it's obviously been a big shock to you......" He tilted his head suddenly, as he crouched down, starting in recognition. "It's Harold Robinson isn't it?....Bloody hell mate, you seem to be having an unlucky of time of it."

Harry seemed surprised at his concern on realising this was DS Radford's officer. "Er...yes....I think I can safely say....... I've had better weeks."

"Why don't you two gents step out from the vehicle, just get a few minutes fresh air and I'll pop back over and see you in five." DC Scott suddenly felt a bit guilty. Kenny had given the poor sod a real grilling and now they knew it wasn't him. This wasn't good.

Mal and Harry watched as Doctors, police, white suited SOCOs, cameras flashing, photographed the scene. "What age do you reckon he was?" Mal whispered.

Finally, the funeral directors went in with a body bag and stretcher trolley. Suddenly, as they began to place bags over the hands, the hood slid from the head as they lifted the body. Harry lurched forward.

"Jeeez Mal! I've seen him before!" Mal looked concerned. "Hang on mate, no, no.....you must be confused...how...where?" By this time DC Scott was on his way back over to them.

"Are you okay Mr Robinson, you seem.......do you want to take a seat."

Harry looked straight at the officer. "Please, can I just take a closer look at the lad, I'm sure I saw him...last night...he bumped into me..." Mal looked distraught.

"Harry man, don't make things any worse..." Then he bit his lip and looked away.

DC Scott waved at the funeral directors to stop and took Harry forward. Harry leaned in slightly, the zip of the body bag was pulled down enough for Harry to see the thin, blood covered face. Yes, it was the lad that had appeared from the shadows, when he was on his way to the pub. Why......how did this happen. Harry just couldn't get his head round this at all.......he felt sick, no worse....he felt scared....really scared....was this just coincidence....what was happening.

Harry hung his head in resigned exhaustion, as DC Scott took him towards a waiting police car. "We'll just take a statement Mr Robinson, standard procedure....just some details...get a picture of what happened last night."

DC Scott wasn't sure whether he should hand-cuff him, he appeared to be coming quietly enough. This would please Kenny anyway. Robinson may not be a murdering pervert......but just a murderer would do Kenny.

Beth could hear loud whispering, several phones were ringing, the office was suddenly buzzing. Two of her officers appeared.

DC Peel came towards her. "Which do want first Sarg....the good news...or the bad news?" She could see by the look on their faces she'd regret hearing either. She rolled her eyes.

"Whatever comes first Peely, what have you got." She watched DC Grant unfold a couple of pieces of paper.

"They're bringing in a possible murder suspect...only it's not for Doris Linton ...they've found a body in an alleyway off Warren Street in the town."

Beth jumped in quickly. "Well, they can't expect us to deal with it, we can't do both...they'll have to get another team up and running."

"Er...Sarg...the suspect, for the what they think is........a possible murder is......Harold Robinson...you know.....the bin-man....DC Scott is bringing him in....."

"Oh! Might have bloody well known it would be one of Radford's lot! Is he going to just have the poor bloke wheeled in every time there's a body found, till he can pin something on him? He just can't let it lie......the arrogant, jumped up tit!"

The two officers shuffled awkwardly at Beth's outburst. She checked herself. It was rare she lost her temper, not a good example to set. She certainly shouldn't take it out on those who didn't warrant her anger.

"Oh...I'm sorry lads...Right....Have we got an ID for the body? Do we know why Mr Robinson is a suspect to this........ possible crime?"

Peely spoke cautiously. "Well...as yet, we haven't been notified of the body ID...but apparently, Harold Robinson and his work associate, Malcolm Gibson found the body." He took a step back to await the reply.

Beth took a few moments, took a deep breath and composed herself.

"So....we're getting so desperate we're arresting the person who finds the body now are we...that is a classic." DC Grant put a finger up, as if wanting to attract the teachers attention in class.

"Well....apparently....on seeing the face....Harold Robinson said he'd seen him last night....he may have been the last person to see him alive, I think that's what DC Scott wants to establish"....

"Oh! I bet he does! Right well...let's not tread on any toes but do a bit of surreptitious digging. Go and speak to Malcolm Gibson, see if you can get any info...you know... last time he saw Harold...state of mind etc. Get him to tell you how they found the body?"

As Beth began to pack away some files and the officers headed for the door, a PC came rushing in. "Message from DI Hayman. Emergency meeting. Any officer on the Linton Murder, need to be at the Incident Room asap, thanks."

The officers looked at Beth. She raised her hands. "I don't believe it, another Emergency Meeting...what's happening in this place? Oh, come on lads...better get to it...asap!"

There was a mad rush for the Incident Room, everyone whispering to each other, as chairs clanked and scraped across the floor. DI Hayman quickly put his jacket on before addressing the officers. Sloppy dress was the sign of a sloppy attitude, even under the sweltering spotlights of the incident room.

He cleared his throat and coughed loudly to get their attention.

"We have had...not sure if you can call it...good news, or bad news. Probably the former if you are relatives of Doris Linton...probably latter if you are the parents of.... Dwayne Prince Dalby". Officers looked puzzled, shrugging shoulders.

"The body found in the alleyway in Warren Street, just over an hour ago, is that of our suspect, for the Linton Murder. He was identified initially by a court letter found in his pocket, for an adjournment from Monday, that letter was dated. LIO gave us a link from the spider tattoo on his forearm. Finally, less than fifteen minutes ago a formal identification was made at the mortuary by his Uncle, Earl Windsor Dalby. So as you can see, we now have a new enquiry......a new dilemma." The DI turned to a PC nearby, who passed over a notebook.

"So far...we haven't had the PM, we have a police pathologist on his way...but have information from the Doctor attending the scene. The male sustained several possible fractures to the leg, arm and head. The head wound being the probable cause of death. Cuts and grazing to the side of the face and what appear to be rodent, or fox bites on the ankle, which considering the body was found in an alleyway with several open bin-bags would not be unusual. We also have another piece of paper, taken from Dalby's trouser pocket which appears to be a note....from his cousin....the 'misper', Liam Dalby. It asks Dwayne to meet him, as he has cash to give him, for him to pay off....a debt collector, known as.... 'Brickhead'. The meeting place stated in the note....Union Street, near the workingman's club. Just a mere stones throw from where his body was found in Warren Street."

The DI is now pointing to an enlarged street map, tapping it vigorously, as if a magician with a wand, hoping for a solution to appear.

"Can we assume Liam Dalby is the killer? He has no previous, but possibly got into an argument with his cousin. Maybe Liam Dalby is our real suspect for the attack on Doris Linton......maybe he was there with Dwayne? He had the cash, Dwayne maybe needed more, maybe he threatened to talk, wanted a bigger payout, remember he had a heavy drug habit. Maybe the moneylender arrived...Dwayne didn't want to let that much money go? Maybe the lender beat up Dwayne in front of his cousin as a warning not to keep the lender waiting for his money......I could go on with the maybes....but what we need are...*facts*...we need cold, hard, evidence."

DI Hayman pulled himself up to his full height, a towering and impressive 6ft 4inches and looked straight out at his officers.

"There are numerous questions to be answered, many actions to follow up. But I have nothing but faith and pride in my officers and know that all of you will do your best. We can no longer ask Dwayne Dalby, the whys and wherefores of the dreadful crime against a frail, elderly lady. We can no longer get the justice that would have been administered if he had been found guilty at a court of law. But....what we can do...for the grieving families...the Beech's' and the Dalby's'.....is get justice.....the truth and a conclusion to this incident. Find Liam Dalby. H*e* is our prime suspect, or our prime concern. He maybe the perp, but he could also, quite easily be......the witness...or ... the next victim......Any questions?"

The room went quiet. Just as officers were about to get up from their seats a voice piped up...it was DS Radford. "We have....Harold Robinson in custody sir.... DC Scott was just about to interview him sir."

The DI looked irritated. "Why Radford, why? He has found two bodies in barely the space of a week...one was a friend and the other in his line of work. I'd say the poor man is unlucky...very unlucky....but being unlucky is not an arrestable offence, even for you Radford."

Radford could hear some officers sniggering, he quickly turned to see Beth staring at him with total disdain, he ignored her, quickly turning back to the DI.

"Actually sir...he knew the second 'victim' as well sir." The DI looked slightly surprised. Radford continued now he'd got his full attention.

"Yes....he told DC Scott at the scene. Said he knew him.... said that he'd, 'bumped' into him earlier last night. Maybe they had an altercation....maybe....he found out Dalby had killed his....'*friend*'." Beth seethed as she heard him emphasise the word.

"Well, Radford......again, we're full of maybes. You do what you have to do but stick to the facts man and not....he said this, he said that. Interview him properly and remember what he's been through, innocent until proven guilty, not the other way round Radford."

"Yes....of course sir...thank you sir."

"Thank you, sir....lick yer boots for you sir....kiss yer arse for you sir...Doesn't he just get right up your nose Sarg?" Beth looked at Pud and whispered. "Well, I have often thought of him as a large bogie you can't get rid of Pud, no matter how often you flick your fingers, so I'm with you on that one. Come on, I need to ring Chappie, give him the update."

273

Beth sat back at her desk, finishing her call. "So, there you have it, it's all happening here, incredible eh!"

Chappie was silent for a moment.... "Well, bugger me sideways! You couldn't make it up, could you? So, I may as well tie things up this end and head back up? I've got an appointment with Dwayne's parents this evening, so I suppose I'll have to break the news to them?"

"I know it won't be pleasant for you, but it has to be done. Thanks Chappie."

"Well from what I've gleaned down here so far, he wasn't exactly the perfect son. Went off the rails at the age of eight, came to Police attention then anyway. Records here show, anti-social behaviour and theft. Then from the age of thirteen he was onto the muggings, burglaries, getting more violent with each crime. In and out the system, parents just seemed to let him get on with it. Mum spent her days in the arcades and bingo, trying to get the big win. Dad, when not, at Her Majesty's pleasure, was usually pissed, or stoned. So, Dwayne's role models weren't exactly your average, hard working, doting parents. You do wonder why they're allowed to breed don't you. Imagine the heartache saved all round if his drugged up, nicotine, raddled, premature body hadn't had an expensive hospital incubator wasted on it. Or am I just being Mr Cynical?"

The line was quiet. "Beth....are you there, are you okay? I didn't mean to depress you. Just hate the sordidness of their squalid little lives. It certainly makes me appreciate my boring, loveless world...eh?" He felt relieved as he heard her laugh.

"It's not loveless…......your moggies adore you!" She concentrated on his humour, she must lighten up, not let it get to her.

"Oh, ay...talking of me moggies, have you managed to nip round and feed them for me, they've had nothing all day and I won't get back up till the early hours...pretty please?"

"Pretty please with a cherry on top?" She teased.

"Eh, you can have my cherry anytime...oooooerrr matron!" He could hear her tutting loudly and could picture her, shaking her head in amused disappointment.

"You...are...so...predictable! Yes...okay...I'll feed your moggies, not sure where I've put your keys though?" She got up, walking towards her coat.

"Well, if you can't find them, there's one under the mat, at the back door." She gasped incredulously.

"Chappie...how many years have you been in the force, how many crime prevention meetings have you attended....and you leave a house key under the mat! Un....bloody......believable!"

"Ah...but....method in me madness...everyone knows about that, knows how silly it would be to leave a key there, so they wouldn't do it, surely. So, no one would bother to look there...Eh! Get me logic? Genius eh!"

"That is the last word that comes to mind......you big buffoon! But I will feed the boys. I've got to nip out between five and six, pop Freddie into the vets...he's got to have his yearly shot and the old worming tablets, so I'll go round after I've dropped him home. I'll have to get off now Chappie, I must be back for the next briefing. We'll see you in the office tomorrow, bright and early?"

"I can do early.......I think bright maybe a big ask. Bye Beth....sorry...SARG!!"

"Bugger off......Detective......Constable......Chapman."

"Is that an order?" She flicked the phone closed, smiling to herself. Typical man always has to get the last word.

"Eh! Sarg...nice bit of technical bling there."

Peely, nods his head in the direction of Beth's girly pink phone, studded with small jewels, she looks embarrassed. "Bit tacky isn't it, it was a pressie, not really my style. Been in a drawer for yonks, but I've lost my other one somewhere, so for now, I shall just have to......get down with the girls in the hood, yo!" She does the crossed, splayed finger gesture. Peely joins in, doing the leg dip walk, as she heads for the door. "Blinging yeah, big up the bling Sarg! Well wicked...innit. See you in sixty Sarg....bayakasha.....baga...sha...." She leaves Peely trying to find his inner Ali G.

Passing the front desk, she sees Scott and Radford heading for the interview room.

Chapter 16

"For the tape. DS Radford and DC Scott are commencing their interview with Harold Robinson at 2.25pm, on Tuesday 21st February 1993 in interview room number three."

DS Radford leans forward slightly. "Are you Harold Robinson?"

"Yes, I am sir." He wanted to add something, but knew whatever he added, with this man, would be just seen as fuel to an already, out of control fire.

"You know why you're here in this interview room, again, Harold?"

"I found the body of a young man this morning, who appears to be a young man who I bumped into last night, when I was on my way to the pub."

"Ah....but you knew the male. DC Scott said you told him you knew the male?"

DC Scott tried to signal and shuffled slightly awkwardly in his seat.

"No.....what I said was that he said, he *recognised* the male, but before last night he'd never seen him before in his life...ever. Next day, there he is...dead...in one of their alleyways, just lying there, amongst the rubbish." Radford glared at Scott

Harry felt truth and emotion would be lost on DS Radford. "So when you said you...'bumped' into him, how hard did you bump into him? Did an altercation ensue?"

Harry gripped his fingers into his knees, to steady his rising anger at the twisting of his words. "I left my home in Essex Street around 9pm-ish. I turned left into Crescent Road." Harold kept his words measured and as precise as he could.

"I'd just passed Surrey Street and was coming up to Kildare Street, when the male, cap on, head down, walking very quickly, came at speed, round the corner and just literally walked into me, his head in line with my chest. We just didn't see each other, it was an accident......pure and simple, an accident. I'll be honest, he didn't seem best pleased, he was a bit agitated, seemed as if he was used to someone probably having a pop at him in that situation." Harold looked straight at DS Radford, knowing what he was thinking, he leant forward a little.

"But....*I...didn't* have a pop at him....I didn't touch him. He just muttered something about me getting in his way, then he just patted me arm and continued on at the same pace, crossing Crescent Road and off down the other half of Kildare. He was fit and well when he walked away from me......."

Harry took a deep breath as DS Radford stayed silent, he continued.

281

"I went to the Westminster....on Parliament Road. My work mates were there, I played darts and dominoes. I was there a good while. If you want to check with staff, I was still there, well after closing. Ay...and before you ask, it wasn't a stoppy-back, nothing illegal. I was waiting for an ex who'd been in touch on the phone earlier. Not that she turned up......got cold feet I expect" Harold looked wistful and a touch disappointed. Before Radford could ask her age and the intimate details of their relationship he continued quickly.

"Beryl, the manageress, made me a cuppa, I hung on till, must have been....gone 11.30pm...ask her. Then the barman, Nick Hobbs, he walked back with me, he lives just down Chester Street, six along from mine...you can ask him as well."

DS Radford didn't want to relent, he didn't believe for one moment that Robinson wouldn't have reacted, knowing what he knew, after all, Dalby had killed his......'friend'. He'd obviously found out from someone.

"So....Harold. You say you did nothing, you didn't follow him, you didn't want to kill him......him......of all people....there right in front of you."

Harold looked confused...what did he mean, what was he talking about...., him of all people, who was he......

"Oh come on man......it seems just too much of a coincidence, somehow you must have found out.... that he'd been there....you knew didn't you....you knew? You were angry! *He* had attacked her...*he* had assaulted her...... well...all but murdered her ......your...... *'friend'*.......Doris Linton."

DS Radford jumped up quickly, his chair falling backwards...that is *not* what he was expecting. Harry had gone a deathly green-grey colour, hauling himself from the table, he tried to steady himself, but couldn't control his body, it lurched forward, a hurting, painful noise rose, crying out, the contents of him spewed across the interview table and down the front of DS Radford. He tried to walk, his body screaming inside, he buckled and collapsed to the floor.

"Aaaaah shit.....Scotty man, look at me bloody shirt! He's hoyed up on me bloody Dolce & Gabbana."

DC Scott stood there in disbelief. "For Christs sake, never mind yer bloody shirt...call the police Doctor...just call a doctor.....*Now*!" Radford not wanting to look as if he were being told what to do, quickly turned to PC Bailey. "You heard him man ...get the bloody doctor!!" He quickly turned off the tape machine and backed from the room.

A police first-aider rushed in, putting Harry in the recovery position, pulling on rubber gloves, clearing vomit from his airways. By this time DS Radford had gone, grabbing a new shirt and tie from his locker, taking spare suit trousers from a hanger. He took the stinking clothes from his body and threw them into a bio-hazard bin. Swearing to himself he went off to the police shower room.

Beth slowly unlocked her front door, balancing the small Jack Russell which was half tucked under her arm.

"Sorry about this little buddy." Freddie looked dejected, as she carried him through to the kitchen and set him down gently in his, fur lined dog bed. "See if we can't find you something to take away the sight and pain of the big man with the needle."

Beth reached into a top cupboard. Freddie's tail began to wag slightly. She wasn't forgiven but this made the discomfort a little more   bearable.

"There you are little fella, a couple of your favourite marrow biccies. Now be good, I've got to go, I've got some, C...A...T...S to feed." She had a feeling her last remaining silk cushion would be in shreds by her return, later that evening.

As she pulled out of Adcott, onto Hall Drive, then took a left up Acklam Road, she thought how strange it was that she'd never been to Chappie's house, neither him to hers. Police socialising seemed to be confined to the Police bars at the bigger stations, or pubs where officers frequented. The 999 parties were great, as were the Christmas parties. But very few entertained at home. Maybe it was the thought of letting their guard down, revealing the person behind the uniform, because more often than not, it was two quite different people. In the force, you had set ideals, set prospects, set values and more importantly, you weren't allowed public opinions.

But behind your own closed door, sod 'em, well to a point anyway!

She turned into Malvern Drive, opposite the cemetery, made her way to the top, curving left into Cradley Drive, nice quiet road, similar houses to hers really. She peered out into the fading light, pulling up slowly outside. The garden seemed very neat. Wonder if he does it himself. She smiled as she pictured Chappie, next to a wheelbarrow full of cats, in an old sweater, picking out the weeds.

Sure enough, at the back door, under the mat, was....the key. She flicked her eyes skywards and unlocked the back door.

Cats were so different from dogs. Cats cupboard love seemed to know no bounds. Whereas Freddie would be cautious, a stranger with food, he would sit and watch until it was put in his bowl and him verbally encouraged to eat it. But cats, they barely let her get into the door, they swirled, head-butted, squeaked and purred. In and out, round her legs, as she searched cupboards and finally came across the tins of cat food. Her gran had had a big tabby tom, he was spoilt rotten.

"Jeez boys...I know you're hungry, I'm going as quick as I can."

Finally, with three faces in three dishes. She got herself together and gave the kitchen a once over, neat and tidy, amazingly clean. Wonder if he has a cleaner, a 'lady who does' as gran used to say. She smiled to herself. He probably puts everything in the microwave.

She had to have just a little nosey round. Her excuse...she could close the curtains, switch on a lamp, make it look inhabited. She stepped through to the open plan lounge...mmm ...not bad. Soft neutral shades with the odd splash of green, very retro. She then spied the huge tome on the coffee table   and laughed out loud.

288

"You have to be kidding me Chappie... War and Peace! Never in a month of Sundays!" There was a bookmark in it, she'd check where he'd got to, quiz him and catch him out, no way was he reading this. She pulled open the cover, her other hand going towards the bookmark. Then she laughed even louder...

"Might have known...a Chappie classic...perfect!"

The huge book had had the middle cut out of its pages, making a huge rectangular secret well full of......chocolates. She unwrapped one, popping it into her mouth she found herself whispering. "My kind of man. Animal lover, sense of humour *and* chocolates, nice one."

Minutes later, as the bowls were emptied, the cats sauntered through, their tails up, allowing her to stroke them as they passed, to their respective resting places. She checked their name tags, as she tickled their chins. Harpo a moth-eaten old ginger tom, made his way to the bean-bag by the radiator. Beth put her hand on it, lovely and warm. The big softie......he sets his heating for the cats. Chico was a rather feisty looking grey short-hair, he jumped with ease, onto the cushioned chair by the desk. Pummelling began, as he circled the cushion several times, before settling down with a positive smile on his face.

Groucho appeared to need a little fuss and reassurance. He looked at Beth blinking and purring loudly. His portly black and white body, reminded her, very much, of Doris Linton's cat. She tentatively and very gently lifted him up into her arms. She hadn't realised just how soft a cat's fur could be. He chucked her chin with his head, in approval of her affection. She put her face against the warm soft body. To her surprise, she felt tears well in her eyes. She felt an overwhelming sadness that kept the tears flowing. The cat seemed to sense her feelings, making small mewing sounds, checking her face and chucking her chin yet again. They stayed close, momentarily, in a mutual understanding of need.

"Silly me, moggies...what was that all about." She gently set the large cat onto to the cushion covered sofa and let him take his pick. He settled quickly, but kept his eyes on her, as she found a tissue, wiped her eyes, checked her make-up, and muttered to herself.

She took a last look at the settled trio and walked from the house, locking the door quietly and carefully replacing the key......back under the mat.

She was smiling again, as she arrived back at the station. But it was short-lived, all hell had broken loose. As she walked towards the main door, an ambulance pulled round the corner. A paramedic rushed through, as she held the door open, another quickly followed with a large bag of medical kit. She went to Millie, on duty at the front desk.

"What on earth is going on....is it someone in the custody suite?"

"No...it's that fella, in the interview room......you know...been in before..Mr Robinson." Millie barely got the words out before Beth was halfway down the corridor.

"PC Southfield! Have you just come out of the interview room?" The PC was just removing his gloves and putting them into a bio-hazard bag. He told Beth all that had happened.

"Is he going to be okay?"

"Paramedic, thinks he's in shock....they're just going to take him up James Cook, check him out...keep him in for obs maybe." Beth peered round the door. "Who's the bloke with him, looks familiar?"

"That's Malcolm Gibson his work-mate, he was waiting for him, to give him a lift home. Seems a decent chap, I had a quick word. He's got a key to Mr Robinsons, says he's gonna feed the cat, get him some clean clothes and drive up the hospital as soon as he can."

"Where the hell is the tactful and oh so subtle DS Radford now? By all accounts we should be able to smell him from here." The PC raised his eyebrows.

"Off like a shot Sarg...like shit off a stick Sarg...if you'll pardon the expression."

"I'll not only pardon it PC Southfield I'll commend it to the house...as a very worthy description."

She patted the PC on the back. "Well done in there...you did a really good job. I'll be putting a note forward to your inspector. Go and get yourself cleaned up and take a well-earned break."

Beth strides back up to the office. "Did you hear it all Pud? Can you believe it...he leaves a man choking on his own vomit, while he goes off and gets a shower......after delivering him that bombshell. The man's a megalomaniac!"

"Apparently he's got an aversion to vomit Sarg."

"Yeh...well I've got an aversion to spiders, but if someone was choking on a pile of them, in front of me, I'd be in there trying to save the poor buggers life, not running away down a corridor squirming like a big girl."

Pud sniggered. "Ay...apparently he did look a bit girly Sarg, according to PC Hall who gave him a wide-birth at the locker rooms."

Beth and Pud spent the next hour putting together some warrants. They really needed to find Liam Dalby, they also needed to rattle some cages. She would have Stacey's place searched, not just for the obvious, Kyle deserved to know he would be protected, one way or the other. They had to try and get an address for Brickhead and associates, also Milo had a couple of properties that might be worth a look.

"Pud, give Mrs. Hocking a ring, she's always been a decent magistrate after hours, she'll usually stop what she's doing and sign a warrant, or two. If she's not available then you could try Mr. Perriman, or maybe Tom Coates. We could do with these warrants being executed early-doors, word will soon get out about Dalby."

An hour and a half later, their last briefing of the day, warrants had been signed and teams put in place. The DI had insisted his officers went home got some well-earned rest and were back in for the searches and their hopeful results. Search officers in at 5am, the rest on duty by 6.30am, searches completed by the briefing at 8am.

Beth had sunk her aching body into a bath of Radox by 10.30pm. Setting her alarm, she climbed into her bed, nudging Freddie over a little with her foot and quickly letting herself succumb to sleep by 11.10pm.

Chapter 17

"Hey...don't all rush at once, I'm back! No really....the applause is enough!" Chappie was bowing, walking backwards towards his desk. "Have you missed me...eh?" This was obviously for Beth's benefit. Without looking up she replied.

"Why, where have you been?" She smiled to herself.

"Hey, I've only had four hours sleep...that's not enough to cope with rejection and humiliation, let me have an hour's kip at me desk then you can throw anything at me."

Beth raised her eyebrows. "You have a kip at your desk now and the only thing being thrown at you will be, a heavy telephone directory, followed by a stapler and an oddly shaped paper-weight! Briefing in ten minutes, let's get our notes together and hope the search teams have something for us."

Peely and Pud handed round teas and coffees and they made their way to the briefing room. The DI was deep in conversation with a couple of the search team sergeants and inspectors. PC Southfield was updating the information board. Pieces of paper and notebooks were being passed from one officer to another. There was an exciting buzz about the room.

Beth sat down slowly, breathing in deeply. What had the searches revealed? Good results, or just more actions and a whole new batch of enquiries to pursue.

"Right, ladies and gentlemen, can I have your attention please. We've got a lot to get through. I need to go through the good and bad of what the searches have turned up."

DI Hayman tried to get his papers in order, then turned to the board.

"Firstly, 104 Granville Road, Grangetown, home of Liam Dalby, also his parents address, Miriam and Earl Dalby and temporary residence to our suspect and now deceased, Dwayne Dalby. Search of this place by Sgt Payne, four PC's and two SOCOs revealed little for the missing male, Liam Dalby. He appears to have taken a holdall and clothing. His mother seemed to think he had gone looking for work, but under the circumstances, he's probably on the run, hiding out somewhere. In Dwayne's room there was residue of drug paraphernalia and several pairs of gloves and screwdrivers. Going equipped stuff in a holdall in the wardrobe. We've sent several items off to forensics."

He turned over several more sheets and continued. "Now to...13 Burns Walk, home of Stacey Lester, Liam's girlfriend and mother of his child, Kyle

Dalby. She also has two other children that appear to stay between hers and her mother's home, 84 Penestone Walk." The DI shuffles slightly and sighs loudly.

"This has been a difficult search for Sgt Walker and her PC's. They had to bring in Social Services after going into the house at 5.30am and finding the boy, Kyle in the bedroom with his Uncle." Beth felt the hairs on the back of her neck rise, she knew what was coming next.

"The brother of Stacey...a Steven Lester, was in the bed with the child. Further searches found child porn amongst other unsavoury DVDs and literature, which would suggest possible goings on, which we will certainly be going through with a, fine-toothed comb and forensics will be doing the same, literally. The child is with social services for the time being and both Stacey and Steven have been brought in for questioning."

Beth sighed heavily, poor little soul, between the devil and the deep blue sea, her intuition had been proved correct, again.

DI Hayman took a couple of quick gulps of strong tea from his mug nearby before continuing. "Two of Milo's properties were searched simultaneously, 97 Union Street and 157 Saltwells Road, by Sgt Richmond and Sgt Peters with eight PC's and four SOCOs. Both houses contained bags of ecstasy tablets, several wraps of heroin at number 97 and some cannabis resin blocks, hidden under the floorboards of number 157 along with what appear to be stolen jewellery and electricals. Both successful in respect of items found, a good haul, but as yet no forth coming information about the fatal assault on Dwayne Dalby and the disappearance of his cousin, Liam. There were large amounts of cash found at Saltwells Road, this maybe drug sales, but could equally be to do with the debt collecting business. We've made several arrests and enquiries are ongoing."

The DI turned, taking a step sideways leaning towards Sgt Morland, a quick whispered exchange, then he turned to face the sea of officers and sighed again.

"Several officers felt a search would be beneficial on the home of Harold Robinson. Mr Robinson is still awaiting release from hospital."

Beth turned to her left and glared at Kenny Radford. Was this the poor man's retribution for puking up over DS Radford. Kenny was such a petty little bastard. She wouldn't be surprised if he didn't get one of his sycophantic, creeping jennies, to plant something in there. Having said that, Julian Morland wasn't a fan of Kenny Radford, by any stretch of the imagination.

"Sgt Morland and officers searched 124 Essex Street thoroughly. They came up with nothing for forensics and nothing of suspicion that would link Mr Robinson to either death. Nothing of interest was found at these premises. Sgt Morland has been in touch with Mr Robinson's workmate, Malcolm Gibson and has arranged for the locksmiths to repair the door asap. His alibi for the evening checks out. Several staff and witnesses saw him in the pub till gone 11.30pm. Also witnesses from the Working Mens Club on Union Street put Dalby very much alive and abusive at around 10pm. So, unless Mr Robinson left his house again after midnight and scoured the streets of Middlesbrough to find Dalby, he is not our man. He had no reason to, he had absolutely no idea who Dalby was until one of our officers decided to enlighten him. We are hoping this will now be an end to Mr Robinsons intrusion, as we feel he can now be eliminated from enquiries at this time."

Much to Beth's relief, the DI looked straight at Kenny Radford and raised his eyebrows. Kenny shuffled awkwardly in his seat. Then the DI looked over, straight at Beth. She sat up straight as if being noticed slacking in class.

"DS Flynn. As you appear to have had the preliminary dealings with the family of Doris Linton, could you pay them another visit? Forensic results show no sign of actual rape, or sexual assault on Mrs Linton, although there was possibly an attempt of some sort. I think we can convey to these decent people that this was a burglary that went wrong, that his attempts to... 'rough her up', threaten, frighten her, got out of hand and that it was this assault that led to her injuries, consequentially to heart failure and death. If it's of any consolation whatsoever, it doesn't appear to have been a premeditated murder. Obviously, you can also let them know the suspect has himself been killed. If you leave the visit till after 1pm, we may have a bit more detail on paper. We don't want them to feel that we can't or won't answer any questions they have. Can I leave that with you Beth? Take a couple of your officers with you."

The DI sighs loudly, rocking slightly. "Well, I think that concludes this briefing. If any officers have any snouts they can get anything from, you know the territory we're in, I don't think anyone is going to be owning up to Dalby's assault, not with a murder, or manslaughter charge on the cards, so we may have to start winding this one down sooner than we think...I'll leave it with you. Next briefing at twelve noon, thank you all for your continued efforts..."

The DI spoke briefly to DS Lawson, then left the room.

"What do you reckon Sarg? Seems a bit swift, talking of winding it down." Beth turned to Pud. "Look at the possible suspects for Dalby. An illegal money lender, that no one dare shop without reprisals, a family that washed their hands of him,

305

several houses full of criminals we've just removed their drugs, cash and belongings from etc. They're not exactly going to be queuing up to, 'assist us with our enquiries,' are they? How many of them will miss him? He owed them more than they owe him. Nobody is going to put themselves in the firing line for a scroat like that, let's be realistic. It'll go quiet pretty quickly, once the press releases the killer of Doris Linton was Dalby, and that he's now dead. People are just going to be relieved he's out the way, after a crime like that."

As she was talking, she caught the eye of DS Lawson and waved him over towards a corner of the room. "Are you dealing with Tracey Lester's children? How bad are things, is it just Kyle, or is that why the older ones preferred to stay at their gran's house?" She couldn't forget the look on that child's face.

"We're not sure about the other two, Social Services and Child Protection officers are with them now.

I think it'll be a slow, painful process. But we do know that the officer who picked Kyle up out of the bed said he was naked and had marks and bruising on his body, including some round his upper thigh and genitals." Beth looked down, her jaw tightened.

"The bastard....and her...his mother, there is no way she didn't know what was going on...how could she let that happen to him......poor little soul...."

DS Lawson leant in towards Beth and whispered. "If it's the last case I do and if it takes me till I retire, I'll make sure Kyle gets justice and that everyone in that prison will be aware of the details of Steven Lester's crimes.... divine retribution...you can't beat it…...well you can, preferably with whatever comes to hand till it squeals for mercy!" Beth squeezed his arm and mouthed thank you. She was choked up. She took a deep breath and headed towards her office.

She slumped down at her desk, physically and emotionally drained, but she had to get herself together, to see the Beech family. She imagined how they were feeling. Guilty, angry, lost, hurt, bereft, disbelieving, how could someone so special to them, be taken from this world in such a cruel, callous and selfish act. What right had that vile piece of shit got, to walk into her normal everyday world and not only shatter it.......but put an end to it. She could feel every ounce of their pain. She closed her eyes tight to stop the tears flowing.

Devine retribution, that's what Adam Lawson had said. That is what Dwayne Dalby had got, you can't do something that wicked and not pay the price. If there was a God.......or any justice in this world then removing the likes of Dalby from it was not going to allow her to lose any sleep.

"You okay Beth, brought you a strong Yorkshire, but while he's parking his truck, you'll have to make do with a mug of tea." Chappie caught her eye.

"You're a life saver, a strong brew, just what we need. Gets us through doesn't it, a stiff upper lip and a strong cup of tea."

"I've got to go back to York, see the Beech family. Won't matter what I say will it, their lives will never be the same, it'll always be there, in the back of their minds....what if we'd... maybe...we should have....she was all alone when....."

Chappie looked at her face, her lashes moist with tears, she was really living this one, she normally kept it together pretty well on these cases.

"Look......if I could go in your place I would, but I've got all the paperwork to go through from Nottingham, intelligence, statements, court files etc."

She visibly straightened, placing both hands on the desk and pushing herself up. "No...no.....I'll be fine, it's my job, my action, another piece of the jigsaw in place. I shall do my best to word it in a way that makes sure, they feel she didn't suffer too much, that she had the heart attack early on, before the worst of the assault, that's if they ask. I'm not volunteering any info on that subject unless they ask. I shall try to give them some solace that justice has been done even if it wasn't in a court of law."

Chappie snorted. "Justice will never be served in a Court of law unless life means life. You know, a life sentence, spending right up until your dying day in prison, being reminded of what you did and why you have been punished. Not languishing at her Majesty's pleasure, with a mobile in one hand and a games consol in the other! It would be a joke if it wasn't so bloody true."

Beth sighed as she put her coat on. "Well, if we weren't here doing what we do, it would be a darn sight worse. We will fight on till there is no fight left in us, that's all we can do......"

Chappie tried to lighten the mood. "By heck lady you'd have been good on the beaches of Normandy with that one! Go and do what you have to do, come back in one piece and I'll treat you to cod and chips later........what d'ya say?"

Beth couldn't help but smile. "I say, make mine Haddock and yer on. I really don't know why you've not been snapped up with offers like that!"

"Hey! Play yer cards right and you might just get mushy peas and a stottie with that, generous to fault me......."

Beth turned and smiled at him as she pulled open the door and disappeared down the stairs to a waiting car. Peely was in the driving seat, he handed her some more paperwork from the incident room, but stayed tactfully quiet. She checked her notes and went over and over the possible questions the family may ask.

Chapter 18

Three hours later, Beth felt drained, she wanted to sit on her hands in the car to stop them shaking, she didn't want Peely to notice her weakness.

It had torn her apart seeing the family suffering so much. They wanted to know, but they didn't want to know, it was all so familiar. Trying to explain the medical findings of the pathologist, but on finding out what it meant they would break down again, gut wrenching sobs she had heard so many times before.

To see those photos all around the room of Doris and family, all laughing in silly Christmas hats. Doris standing between the twins, towering over their little gran. Doris with such pride in her eyes. Those poor boys won't see grans pride on their graduation day. Hetty won't get to give her mum a hug on Mother's Day. All they'll remember is the fear she must have felt in her last minutes on earth and they weren't there for her. Life was cruel, then it twisted the knife, just for good measure.

Peely could see her discomfort, he wasn't good at small talk.

"You'll be glad that's over.... and at least he's out the way as well, can't harm anyone else now can he......at least that's something Sarg."

"Yeah......at the very least, that's something. Don't honestly think the Beech family, or anyone else that's suffered at his hands will see it quite like that."

He stared straight ahead, feeling his palms sweaty on the steering wheel. It hadn't come out quite how he'd meant it to, he tried again.

"No but, at least they don't have to get dragged through the courts with him. You know he'd have pleaded not guilty. It would have been a nightmare in court, all the details being read out.... you know…..."

She gave him a half smile to acknowledge his effort at understanding.

"Yes, the only right thing he did in his vacuous, selfish, violent little life was die, giving Doris and her family just a final little glimpse of decency and release not having to be hauled through the courts and having to see that shifty little scroat pleading 'Not Guilty' and trying to lie his way out of it all."

The DI was doing a final briefing at 6pm. Beth took her time getting back to the office. She stood quietly in the corner of the Police yard. She took a few deep breaths and felt a little light-headed, steadying herself she placed a hand on the wall. Was it nearly over, had she come through it. She didn't want to queer her pitch. It was nearly two years since she'd moved up here. She hoped she'd made her mark, done things right. She had some good officers, good friends. She had made some difficult decisions, she hoped they were all for the right reasons.

She went upstairs, straight to her desk, quickly wrote up some notes from her visit to the Beech family. She enquired with Emma, the CID Clerk as to the whereabouts of DC Chapman and DC Ambrose. Emma told her they were clearing a couple of late actions and had said they'd be back for the briefing. They were cutting it fine as Beth could see officers already making their way up the corridor.

She got up, straightening her skirt, slipping her aching feet back into her shoes she picked up her

316

notebook, some relevant paperwork and got herself to the briefing. Sitting herself down on the second row, she could hear the boys chatting as they came in minutes later, but there was only standing room left.

DI Hayman looked remarkably fresh, probably had a large lunch and a cat-nap, he was laughing and joking with a couple of PCs, before stepping forward and clearing his throat loudly.

"Can I have your attention......please!" The general chatter ceased.

"I have had a couple of meetings this afternoon with various bodies, including the press, Social Services and my superiors."

There was a spattering of noise. DI Hayman raised one eyebrow. It did look slightly comical, but they knew not to laugh.

"This has been an unusual case, or case within a case really. Not taking for granted the events of the last week or so, we have managed to tie up a couple of actions and loose ends this afternoon, which has helped enormously with the progress of this case and other crimes which have come to light through the work done by yourselves and associated officers." He turned slightly.

"Right, Sgt Morland and WPC Khan." Both officers step forward. Julian Morland took a quick look at his notes then spoke.

"We have Steven Lester in custody, charged with indecent assault on a minor. He'll be up at Court tomorrow and hopefully detained, pending forensic evidence." Julian then caught Beth's eye. "We will also be charging Stacey Lester with wilful neglect. We will be speaking to her again in approximately an hour, she became abusive and hysterical during questioning, so we're giving her a break and the Police Doctor is on   his way to check her over".

318

WPC Khan takes some papers from him, then hands the Sgt a large file, which he opens carefully.

"Social Services now have all three children and they will be placed with emergency foster carers until the situation at home has been assessed. Sadly, this is a copy of the Social Services file, so as you can see, there had been ongoing problems, but apparently nothing serious enough to bring them to police attention. Whether they didn't have the evidence to act until now, who knows. Investigations are being made. All three children have been seen by a doctor. The youngest girl, Teegan has some old bruising and a scar on her lower back. Kyle.......has more recent injuries, significant bruising over several areas of his body and tearing around the anus, this is one frightened, confused and traumatised little boy. Needless-to-say, Child Protection officers are being passed this file and will be spending time with these children over the next few days, weeks and no doubt months, whatever it takes to

319

help them through their ordeal. Other family members and associates of the Lesters are also being spoken to. This has obviously come to light due to our enquiries for the 'misper' Liam Dalby. Although this has been harrowing for all concerned it is only due to the vigilance of officers that this is being dealt with.......who knows what we could have found six months, or a year on from now if we hadn't intervened........So, thank you for all you hard work."

Beth's eyes said it all as Sgt Morland turned away to join the WPC who was now sitting back with other officers.

The DI thanked the officers then tilting his head back slightly, he let out a long sigh before continuing.

"This has certainly been a trying time for many, you open up that can and the worms come spilling out, sometimes you wonder if they'll ever stop. But that's why we're here, it's what we do......irradicate the worms. Pull them wriggling from their lairs and sort the good from the bad and the bad from the evil. I think most of you will agree when I say I believe Steven Lester and Dwayne Dalby to be the latter. Although many will feel he got what he deserved. An eye for an eye, a death for a death. We could say that whoever, assaulted him has done us all a favour ....but...........he was still a human being....albeit only just."

The DI left a gap knowing there'd be whispered comments, such as... 'that's debatable sir' or.... 'spawn of the devil more like.'

"I know…...I know, but we are doing our job and investigations are going well for all concerned. Moving along quickly, I have an update on the, afore mentioned 'misper', Liam Dalby. He contacted his mother, Miriam. She updated him on Dwayne's death, so he went with his boss straight to the nearest police station front desk. He gave his whereabouts at the time of Dwayne Dalby's death. He had in fact gone to Newcastle as his mother had mentioned, for a labouring job and his new boss confirmed this. The good news for Mr Liam Dalby was that he has not been charged with anything. Sadly, the bad news for him was that his son was possibly being abused by his girlfriend's brother. Needless-to-say, it was fortunate his mother didn't want to give him this news over the phone and that he was in a police station with understanding officers at the time. Had he been here I feel we would have at least another double murder on our hands. He was distraught, as one can imagine, but if nothing else, when the investigation is over the little lad will hopefully end up in a happier environment with a parent who cares and wants to protect him."

The DI takes a slight step back. Beth now feels he's earned that large lunch and catnap. He raises a hand to quieten down the chatter.

"Okay....okay...we have a lot to get through....can we now have an actions update from....DC Chapman and DC Ambrose . Anything else come to light lads?"

Chappie mouthed, 'sorry' at Beth as he walked past her chair to the front of the room, she looked puzzled.

"DC Ambrose and I got a couple of actions handed to us, just after the Sarg left for York. We went to see a Reginald Boyland, lives in Warren Street. He was returning from a couple of days away, he's a HGV delivery driver, so didn't catch up with the news till he was reading the Gazette last night. He wasn't sure if what he had to tell us was significant, neither are we to be honest. He'd just been dropped off at the end of his road, around 10.20pm. He said he was tired and not really alert and he assumed it was just kids, druggies, alchies hanging around in the streets near the alleyways. He said, there's always people lurking about in the shadows, the noise goes on most of night, he just got used to it. There was no way he'd take a look, or check anything out, not worth it. He went to unlock his door. But just as he did, he heard someone shout, it was a low whisper. He wasn't sure how close it was as voices seem to carry in the night. He thinks someone was calling to a mate......or an accomplice maybe? He said it sounded like the words......"Come here! Leave him......Eddie, or Jeddy......He said the voice was then muffled and it all went quiet."

DC Ambrose then took over. "We've been down and checked out Local Intelligence and it could one of two males. Edward 'Eddie' Fraser, coincidently, one of Miles 'Milo' Harrisons muckers and partners in crime. Also, there is a, Gerald 'Jed', possibly 'Jeddy' to some, Jameson. Jed is a debt collector for the big man, Brian Coleman, alias 'Brickhead'. We've spoken to both and it's 'no comment' from all concerned. Without evidence it's just supposition. We know they would have good reason to want to hurt Dalby, probably a warning that went wrong, but whether we get anywhere with it is another matter."

Chappie now looking straight at Beth, pulled out another piece of paper from his pocket. She looked at him quizzically, tilting her head slightly.

"The other action was from a Mrs Ivy Elliot, a friend of Doris Linton. She left a message saying she had a note for DS Flynn." Beth was now frowning looking a little worried that she'd missed something important from Mrs Elliott.

"So as DS Flynn was down in York, we did her a favour and popped along to collect it. It's just the name and telephone number of the eliminated, 'man in black.' Mrs Elliot said she didn't know if you needed to speak to him again, just in case.......she's written down his name and number."

Beth got the message loud and clear and raised her eyebrows in that, 'don't you dare say anymore' look. Chappie and Ambrose were trying to keep a straight face as they handed her the note.

"You know exactly where that Haddock is going later don't you?" She growled under her breath.

"Promises, promises, I've never had an aversion to a slap with a wet fish."

He moved quickly passed her as the officers nearby chuckled in amusement.

Even the DI was smiling at the welcome, relaxing intrusion.

"Well, we may not have caught the killers of Dwayne Dalby, but more importantly, we may have a date in the offing for our lovely DS Flynn."

She blushed with embarrassment, as she heard a wolf-whistle and some laughter, but she did also tuck that piece of paper safely in her pocket.

"Right....we've had our fun....let's get focused again, let's not forget why we're here. We're here to do a job and I think you have all pulled out all the stops on this one. This has been a difficult case from the moment we found Doris Linton's body. We have covered everything, we've found what we needed and more, I can't thank you enough for all your hard work on this case.

He sighed loudly again, looking down for several minutes, then he turned to the work boards full of photos, lists, names and information.

"But, ultimately, all this work doesn't get you a suspect if no one talks and you have no forensics. For Doris Linton we have and that is a major relief for us and for her family, but for Dwayne Dalby I feel we will be waiting a long time for anyone to care enough to bother. I think we can safely say that whoever he owed took what little they could in retaliation, that being his pathetic, violent, wasted little life. Milo's lads are not going to come forward, 'Brickhead is not going to compromise himself in any way by giving us anything, so I think this will be our last, full compliment briefing. Uniform will be vigilant on the streets and continue asking questions to associates etc and we'll take it down to six CID officers......DS Tranter and his officers will keep it going for the time being. Just leaves me to say thank you to you all, I am so enormously proud of all the officers and civilians that have been involved. I shall be winding down in the police bar in about an hour if anyone would like to join me. Go and get yourselves a well-earned rest."

You could visibly see the whole room relax, smiles on faces, the patting of backs. It was a horrendous crime, it had been a difficult time, but they had done their jobs, they had done all they were capable of doing to make things right. They had every reason to feel good. Because they knew that no sooner had this one been laid to rest, they would be called to another. So, they didn't need to be asked twice to have some time out. There are only so many wounds, dead bodies, distraught relatives, 'no comment' suspects and crime scenes you can cope with seeing without rest and recuperation in between.

"Yeah, party on dudes...I'm off to the bar are you lot coming down?"

Pud was doing a strange little shuffle dance, his face lit up like a child. Peely chuckled as he clicked his phone shut. "Not me mate....I'm on a promise... Just texted me lady, she's putting something in the oven which will take exactly an hour and thirty and asks if I can think of anything, we can do in the time....wahayyyy!"

Chappie winked at Beth before turning to Peely. "That'll be the 1000-piece jigsaw of the Pembrokeshire Coast then Peely....eh?" They all laughed as he dashed from the room. "Yer just jealous, just cos' I'm getting some...."

"Yes, we are ...I like a good Hotpot!"

They wandered back through to the office. Chappie spoke, tentatively.

"Are we still on for fish and chips tonight, Beth?"

"Yes, that would be great, I'm starving! I'll get me self home, give Freddie a quick jog around the block......would 8pm be okay?"

"Round at yours, I'll collect the food on the way?" He looked sideways.

"Brilliant, I'll do a bit of bread and butter and a cuppa."

"I thought you might want to ring someone else to share fish and chips with?" He thought he'd test the water, risk the stapler being thrown his way.

"Funny....funnnnnnyyyyy! Don't push it Mr if you know what's good for you, like I said before, I will be armed with a Haddock and I won't be afraid to use it." She grabbed her coat and bag and headed for the door, then turned.

"See you at eight....and if you really want to get into my good books you could get Freddie a small, battered sausage." She grinned.

"Hey...I have a small, battered sausage of my own......if you want..."

"Don't even go there....because I definitely won't be going there, but I can always set Freddie on it....."

"Ouch! No thanks...... message understood...... over and out."

It's not that she didn't like Chappie, he was a good man, a funny man, just too close for comfort. A DS with a DC, in the same team, not appropriate....at all. But, in the future, if one of us applied elsewhere, or even moved   departments…...or   moved divisions…...maybe...something   could   happen…...she sighed heavily….

Or maybe not…….

Chapter 19

She threw her old tracksuit on and took Freddie round the block, then jumped in the shower. Quickly drying her hair, she left it loose and threw on some soft brown trousers and green polo shirt. She just wanted to be comfortable and relaxed. She did flick a layer of mascara on though and a slick of lipstick......and a light spray of Chanel's 'Chance'......

She was just putting the plates on trays when Freddie bounced from his bed on hearing a knock at the door. "Come here...Leave it...Freddie!" She rushed to grab him just in case he bolted when the door opened.

Chappie was standing there looking a little ashen. Beth was concerned.

"What's happened, are you okay?"

He gathered his thoughts and proffered the large bag of food.

"Er...yes......honestly I'm fine... nearly ran over a hedgehog coming round that last corner, just bumped the kerb, you know what I'm like about animals...."

Beth smiled. "Ah...you big softy...come in, I'll serve it out before it gets cold. Go through take a seat. Gosh....there's loads in this bag, you'll have to take a 'catty-bag' home for the moggies if we don't finish it all."

Chappie looked around the neat, neutral coloured lounge, with its, splash of colour paintings, stylish oak furniture and big soft, pale chairs. He noticed a couple of photos in striking silver frames. Beth with......her parents he presumed and the other with her arms wrapped around an elderly lady with a sweet, smiley face. It made him smile too. He was close to his family as well. Mum's Sunday dinners were legendary.

"Coming through, fish and chips twice, mushy peas, stottie and a cup of Yorshire tea......how spoilt are we?" Beth put the huge tray down on the coffee table then nipped back for a couple of lap trays.

"Good job we're both starving, look at all that?"

"Well, I tried to ring you on me mobile, but I think 1 must have dialled the wrong number ." Then he noticed the pink sparkly phone on the arm of her chair.

"No......you'll be ringing my old phone I lost it, had to use this thing all week.....not really me, but needs must."

They both tucked into their food with relish, with Freddie, crinkly eyed, looking from one to the other after wolfing down his sausage treat in about five seconds flat. Chappie glanced at Beth, she looked cute with her hair all dishevelled ....and she smelt gorgeous.

"That's a lovely photo over there, with your....is it your nanna?"

"Yes, I called her gran, grandma.......nanna's more local to this area."

"Where were you from…...Midlands, Derby, Mansfield, Nottingham way?" Chappie kept his eyes towards the photo.

"Outskirts really, I came up here from Midland Street Station, Long Eaton. I needed a change. I'd passed my sergeants' exams and I just wanted the experience. I wasn't really bothered where it was."

Beth left some of her food and took her tray into the kitchen. She shouted through to Chappie who was just squeezing in the last couple of mouthfuls.

"There's a nice photo of my parents, gran and me on the sideboard at the other end of the room......my graduation, at least she got to see that." He could hear her voice falter.

337

Beth came back through to the lounge, as Chappie was just replacing the photo onto the sideboard.

"Gran passed away I'm guessing?"

"You know……you're not guessing."

Beth sat down heavily into the chair. Chappie perched on the end of the settee pressing the buttons on his mobile. Ironically, they both heard the tune of the 'Sting' coming from the far drawer of the nearby unit.

Beth spoke unconvincingly. "Oh…….that's where it is. That's the first thing I should have done with the pink one isn't it, dial the number to find it."

Chappie slumped down into the settee and slowly brought his hands down across his face and sighed heavily.

"I never did share with you what I found in Nottingham did I?"

"What about, Dwayne Dalby? What did you find? Apart from a history of, theft, violence, burglary, assault, what else is there? Like the DI said, he was just pure evil."

"Absolutely!......Not doubting that for a minute. A shitty little specimen, that got worse with age. Two violent muggings under his belt by fourteen, continually terrorising the residents of Bulwell. His parents couldn't have cared less about him, or what he was doing. Then he was dossing around in bedsits, eventually ending up with three others in a squat in Sneinton near the centre of Nottingham, his drug habits escalated and he knew how to get easy money.......target the elderly."

Beth bit her lip. She was staring straight ahead, then turned back to Chappie. "Go on......What else did you find out about, Dwayne Dalby?"

"That the courts continually released him, with either little or no evidence, he got fines, curfews and bail, always bail. Two elderly

339

ladies had their bags snatched, one falling to the floor and breaking her hip. Artists Impressions and ID parades, with their poor eyesight gleaned little. Then he began the burglaries. Two in Carlton, one burglary and two attempt breaks in Woodthorpe. But his second in Mapperly took him higher up the bad to evil scale. I read the files and recognised the MO. Small downstairs transom window, inverted glove marks, 1 saw the book of forensic scene photos, the 'Peoples Friend' magazine on the coffee table. What Dwayne hadn't bargained for was a tiny feisty poodle trying it's best to protect its owner…...fighting to the last, barking out a warning. The case photos show it with horrific injuries, kicked to death, then probably stamped on for good measure."

Chappie knew he had to continue. Beth now had her eyes closed her arms locked around her knees. She opened them as he stopped talking.

"When did you know, what did I do that gave it away…...how...?"

"It was the death certificate. When I realised the elderly lady had died the same night after an assault, I just wanted to see if she had had a weak heart like Doris Linton, or whether…...I never thought....The ladies name was, Elizabeth May Peacock, it didn't click till I saw her daughter-in-law's name, there on the certificate.......Georgina May......Flynn."

Tears streamed through Beth's tightly closed eyes.

"And your name, from the graduation photo over there with the certificate.... Elizabeth May Flynn.........the victim in Mapperley was your gran?"

Beth swallowed hard, almost choking on the tears. The relief that someone knew...... that she could tell someone what had happened......the truth.

"I had heard of Dwayne Dalby when I worked on the outskirts of Nottingham, I was in uniform for a few years in Mansfield. It was usual everyday police work. The usual suspects, crimes, searches, arrests. Then I decided to do my Sergeants Boards and I was transferred to Sherwood as Acting Sgt. I was married by then, so I was Acting Sgt Franks. That's when Dalby first came to my attention, along with some other druggies, that were mugging, robbing and thieving in the area. He was such a cocky little shit. He didn't care about anything or anyone. I'd already taken the statement and been with SOCO when they were taking the photos of Margaret Hudson, the lady who fell during the bag snatch and broke her hip. The fear in her eyes when she talked about him, she'd been traumatised."

Beth leaned forward in her chair towards Chappie, she clutched at her knees again. "You can't describe how useless you feel when you know who it is and you can't nail them. We had officers raiding every squat in Sneinton. We got stolen property, drugs, drug paraphernalia, weapons and cash by the bag load. We got thieves, burglars, prostitutes and Dwayne Dalby. The usual solicitor gets him off on a technicality and he walks, with a smug smirk on his ratty little face. Then two weeks later we get a shout that an elderly lady has been found dead, possible burglary and assault. I just went to do my job......I had no idea...they had no idea, then the address comes over the radio......54 Sandford Road....a bungalow...Porchester Road end....it just didn't register at first.....

Chappie put a hand towards Beth, but she just kept her arms clamped around her knees. "Look if it's too upsetting......you don't have to......"

"My parents faces......can you imagine.....they'd found her...she had an opticians appointment that morning. They'd realised as soon as they walked in, mum was nearly sick when they saw little Humphrey's crushed and bloodied body, dad rushed through calling to Betty......then he found her......like broken doll. All her belongings, all her little treasures...the little boxes she'd let me open as a child... full of beads and pretty buttons.....her dance shoes...gold and sparkly....all her special things her memories thrown everywhere...even on top of her. Just as if she was a bit of discarded rubbish......never ever will I forget that sight, as long as I live. Those huge, dark bruises, the purple welts of fist against flesh, the twisted limbs hanging down from her pretty, pink bedspread. How could another human being take pleasure from inflicting such fear and pain on someone so vulnerable and helpless."

Beth sighed, pulling herself upright, then leaning back in the chair, her hands now loose and resting on her lap.

"The officers suddenly realised what relation I was to the deceased and removed me from the scene along with mum and dad. They quickly had me transferred to Long Eaton, the other side of the city and insisted I have time off, counselling, all the usual stuff. I spent most of that time just being a bereaved granddaughter. That's when my husband decided to stay with a.......'friend'. We lived in Ruddington, mum and dad only lived up from gran in Carlton...it was too much for them and we had a big house... I had them to stay for awhile...we needed to be together. It all just fell apart, my family.......my marriage.....my world....all because of that little piece of shit."

Chappie sat back as well, he just had to let her talk, however heart-breaking it was to hear. "How did you know it was Dalby?"

"They matched fibres from his jacket, he'd ripped it on the transom window catch on an attempt burglary the night before, in Hilton Road, it was only the next road down. The windows were the old-fashioned metal ones, bit smaller than the new ones, it was a bungalow though and home to an elderly couple. He obviously decided to come back. He'd be desperate not getting anything the night before. He was found four days later, hiding in one of the sheds on the allotments backing on to the recreation ground up towards Colwick Reservoir. He was interviewed, went 'no comment', then to 'not guilty'. Got him to court, the Solicitor got him to admit to the attempt burglary, knowing we had forensic, then not guilty on several other breaks including my gran's home........We'd had the post-mortem results, almost word for word like poor Doris Linton......she had a heart condition. She didn't die from her injuries... but she'd suffered a violent beating.... a sexual assault...... the indignity of such a vile attack at 80 years old........you just can't imagine the fear she went through, the pain...the trauma....to be so terrified that your heart just screams out, no more.........and just stops."

Beth's eyes were streaming with tears, she reached for a box of tissues from a nearby table and pulled out a handful before continuing.

"I had a friend, a WPC, she kept me informed after the case, she let me know where Dalby was, if he was detained for anything, if he moved squats etc. Then she said he'd gone off the radar. By then I was looking to get some experience in CID and as time passed, I got Acting DS at Wollaton Road Station, as luck would have it, there was a load of new officers and transfers, a lot I didn't know, so I just got on with the job. We had several burglaries in the area so could glean intelligence to assist with our enquiries. We had a couple of breaks with a similar MO that Dalby used, so I had the excuse to ask family and associates where he was. His family were never at court, so to them I was just a 'pain in the arse' copper harassing them. So, when I asked if they knew where he was, they were more than happy to get me off their doorstep and out of their sight by telling me he'd....'Gone up North', to fleece off his Uncle, Earl Dalby.' It wasn't difficult finding that family and once I'd sorted out a transfer for my all-important promotion, it all slotted into place. I missed mum and dad so much but I had to bide my time......I had to get it right......I knew he would continue up here....too much temptation...but it didn't go to plan...how could it..... how could you predict the mind of pure evil."

Chappie looked a little worried now and didn't quite know what was coming next. He almost jumped from the settee as Beth got up suddenly, lunging forward and grabbing the cups. "I'm sorry I really need another cup of tea, you might decide it's my last, so I need a good strong brew, if I'm to continue with this."

"Never mind tea Beth, I think I need the small room, I nearly had an accident then, you put the fear of God into me!" They quickly did what they had to do and returned to the comfortable seating.

"Look Beth, I think I know where this is going..."

"Yes....and it's because you think you know where it's going, I have to tell you the truth. Dalby had been doing shed breaks over South Bank way, bit of shoplifting, I was sure he was ready for something bigger, I knew from drugs intelligence, who he was buying from, I knew the set-up at Granville Road. His Uncle hated his guts, his Aunt thought he was a bad influence on their son, Liam. It was only a matter of time before he moved on and for that he needed a decent amount of money......I had planned to just have him beaten up by the henchmen......but then the death of poor Doris Linton brought it all flooding back. Then the results came in, same MO, same cause of death, he'd get off yet again....

I had to make sure his victims got justice, I had to......Of course I didn't count on Kenny Radford getting a bee in his bonnet about poor Harry Robinson, I had to make sure everyone would know it wasn't him......I gave him the alibi......I felt dreadful doing it because I betrayed his trust with information that he'd given me. Before I took his keys back, I had an extra set of alley keys cut. I asked him about his life and routines, we had a natter about stuff over a cuppa, including about his ex-girlfriend Jilly. I knew he'd be in the pub Monday night, so I rang from the pink phone, not traceable as mine. I stood next to a busy road, with noisy traffic and spoke quietly, saying it was Jilly and would he wait at the pub for me, as I'd heard about what had happened, just wanted to talk. He heard what he wanted to hear and waited, till well after 11pm. I'd also known from checking LIO that Dalby had a Court appearance on Monday morning. It was a long shot he'd turn up......but he knew what he'd done, better to turn up for that than stay away and have them come and ask questions when arrested for a bench warrant."

Chappie was now intrigued. "But we had him in on the Monday after his Court appearance, I didn't see you take him to one side, or anything?"

"It had already been set in motion. We knew Liam Dalby was missing... so I wrote the note from Liam, telling him to meet, to collect the money. I hovered outside the court before I came into the office. I saw a court clerk I recognised and just said I was in a rush could they give this to reception for the named to receive on their arrival."

Chappie pulled a face....... "Risky that mind...."

"I know but it had to be that night, it had to tie up and I knew greed would take over and he'd be there. But it nearly backfired, l couldn't believe he *bumped* into Harry. He must have still been dossing at the Parker's house.....and then for poor Harry to be the one to find the body next day. I'm only grateful Kenny Radford was the buffoon on his case...talk about, hoist by his own petard. Before I tell you the final piece, which I think you know...I need you to tell me something. Why were you the colour of cold clay when I opened the door tonight? Much as I know you love wildlife and animals in general, you looked more like you'd seen, or heard a ghost, not a hedgehog...?"

Chappie picked up his tea, took a sip not taking his eyes from Beth.

"I suddenly realised it was too much of a coincidence after today...speaking to Mr Boyland who'd heard the whispered shouts that night. 'Come on!.....Leave him!....Eddie...or Jeddy......or was it Freddie? I heard you shout virtually the same words tonight as Freddie ran to the door......That and the Nottingham connections and the death of your gran.......it was you wasn't it?"

Beth sighed, with tiredness and relief to be sharing her guilt, finally.

"It was easy to lure the scroat across the road and to the alley, I'd already unlocked the gate with the duplicate keys, he could see the money, then when he put his hand out to take it, I just grabbed him round the neck quickly to turn him away, twisted his arm up his back and hit him several times. Freddie was fastened in a backpack I'd put down nearby with a change of clothes......I'll be totally honest and I know you probably won't believe me, but I hadn't meant to kill him. Something inside me thought maybe, just maybe, if he feels real fear and pain, he'll consider what he's inflicted on others and he may stop. But then he pulled a knife, it was my turn to feel fear. I knew I was bigger and stronger than him...but with a knife...he was going mental... slashing at me, he cut the side of my coat and caught my thigh, it stung like hell. Freddie must have seen the knife...he broke free from the bag, leapt at him and was caught in the belly...hence me

353

saying I was taking him to vets for his jab etc. It was a check up and antibiotics.

Chappie looked stunned. "You could have been killed......both of you."

"He'd never used a knife on anyone before, how was I to know he'd have one with him that night. Freddie bit his ankle and pulled him off balance, that's when he fell and lost the knife and I saw red, I thought of my gran and Doris and I just kept hitting him and whacked him so hard his head just slammed against the wall and he slumped into the rubbish......right where he belonged. I picked up the knife, called to Freddie and we disappeared.......I'm no better than he is, am I?"

Chappie was now standing, he held out his hand and pulled her up. She knew this was it. He would have to take her into custody. Her parents would see her in court after all that they had been through......Oh God what had she done....   She stood there, tears streaming down her face......her whole body shaking.......but Chappie didn't read her her rights, he just took her in his arms and held her....tightly. Then he spoke.

"You didn't kill him. It was an accident during a beating. Everyone assumes that Dalby was beaten up for not paying his debts, for treading on toes of the drug dealers and generally being a nuisance to all who knew him. The people who suffered in all this have been the victims and their families. Justice couldn't be done for them in a court of law, but it's been more than done by wiping him off the face of this earth to save others. The only people that know exactly what happened that night are you, me and Freddie. I think we can safely say he won't be talking.......so that leaves you and me. As far as I'm concerned you have suffered enough...more than enough and I am not about to bring the rest of your life crashing down around your ears."

Chappie pulled away just enough to be looking her straight in the eyes......large, sad, bewildered and full of tears, she could only gaze at him in stunned silence.

"As our big friendly, neighbourhood and ever helpful bin-man would probably say......we're just.......taking out the trash"..........

THE END